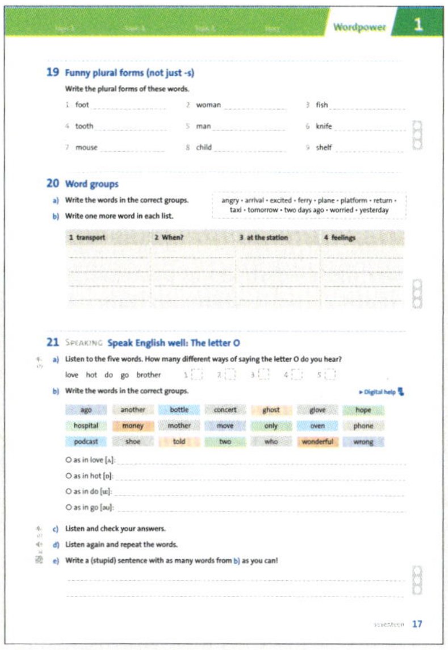

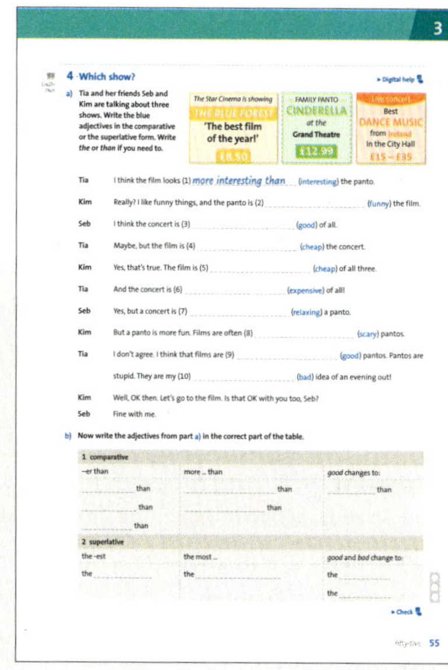

Wordpower

Auf dieser Seite findest du Übungen zu den Vokabeln der jeweiligen Units und kannst dein gesprochenes Englisch verbessern.

My learner log

Hier kannst du auf die Unit zurückblicken und deinen Lernstand festhalten.

Revision

Halte auf diesen Seiten inne und wiederhole, was du in den vorherigen Units gelernt hast.

W0340150

Diese Verweise führen dich in die *Diff bank* am Ende der Unit

▶ More help	▶ Early finisher	▶ Challenge
Hilfen zu den Aufgaben	weitere Übungen	weitere Übungen mit höherem Schwierigkeitsgrad

Dein Buch findest du auch in der Cornelsen Lernen App

Siehst du eines dieser Symbole in deinem Workbook, kannst du in deiner App ...

Erklär-film	▶ Digital help	▶ Check
alle Hörtexte und Videos zu deinem Buch aufrufen.	auf Ideen und Hilfen zugreifen.	deine Antworten eigenständig überprüfen.

lighthouse 2

Workbook Lehrkräftefassung

Im Auftrag des Verlages erarbeitet von
Gwen Berwick, York
Sydney Thorne, York

In Zusammenarbeit mit der Englischredaktion
Klaus Unger (Projektleitung),
Lisa Ahmadi (verantwortliche Redakteurin), Michael Dunkel, Christine House, Chelsea Ledvinka-Heß, Julian Theo Wacker, Karin Wedepohl

Beratende Mitwirkung
Anke Barth, Plauen; Armin Düpmeier, Warendorf; Lara Jano, Rottweil

Medienmanagement
Silke Kirchhoff

Illustrationen
Harald Ardeias, Schelklingen; Irina Zinner, Hamburg

Fotos
Anja Poehlmann, Brighton

Für die freundliche Unterstützung danken wir der *Varndean School, Brighton*

Umschlaggestaltung
Rosendahl, Berlin

Layoutkonzept
Klein & Halm, Berlin

Layout und technische Umsetzung
Straive

Passend zum Workbook:
Sprechen, Aussprache, Wortschatz und Grammatik digital üben mit der mobilen App ChatClass. Erhältlich auch als PrintPlus-Lizenz bei Nutzung des Arbeitsheftes.

www.cornelsen.de

Die Webseiten Dritter, deren Internetadressen in diesem Lehrwerk angegeben sind, wurden vor Drucklegung sorgfältig geprüft. Der Verlag übernimmt keine Gewähr für die Aktualität und den Inhalt dieser Seiten oder solcher, die mit ihnen verlinkt sind.

Soweit in diesem Lehrwerk Personen fotografisch abgebildet sind und ihnen von der Redaktion fiktive Namen, Berufe, Dialoge und Ähnliches zugeordnet oder diese Personen in bestimmte Kontexte gesetzt werden, dienen diese Zuordnungen und Darstellungen ausschließlich der Veranschaulichung und dem besseren Verständnis des Buchinhaltes.

Dieses Werk berücksichtigt die Regeln der reformierten Rechtschreibung und Zeichensetzung.

Alle Drucke dieser Auflage sind inhaltlich unverändert und können im Unterricht nebeneinander verwendet werden.

© 2023 Cornelsen Verlag GmbH, Berlin

Das Werk und seine Teile sind urheberrechtlich geschützt.
Jede Nutzung in anderen als den gesetzlich zugelassenen Fällen bedarf der vorherigen schriftlichen Einwilligung des Verlages.
Hinweis zu §§ 60 a, 60 b UrhG: Weder das Werk noch seine Teile dürfen ohne eine solche Einwilligung an Schulen oder in Unterrichts- und Lehrmedien (§ 60 b Abs. 3 UrhG) vervielfältigt, insbesondere kopiert oder eingescannt, verbreitet oder in ein Netzwerk eingestellt oder sonst öffentlich zugänglich gemacht oder wiedergegeben werden.
Dies gilt auch für Intranets von Schulen.

Druck: ppm Fulda GmbH & Co. KG, Fulda

1. Auflage, 1. Druck 2023
Workbook 2
ISBN 978-3-06-035820-5

1. Auflage, 1. Druck 2023
Workbook 2 Lehrkräftefassung
ISBN 978-3-06-035821-2

PEFC-zertifiziert
Dieses Produkt stammt aus nachhaltig bewirtschafteten Wäldern, Recycling und kontrollierten Quellen
PEFC/04-31-1308
www.pefc.de

Ida-Noddack-Gesamtschule
Martinistraße 12 · 46483 Wesel
Telefon 0281/1649790

lighthouse 2

Workbook Lehrkräftefassung

Audios online verfügbar unter
www.cornelsen.de/webcodes **Code:** mucawu

Dein Workbook findest du auch in der Cornelsen Lernen App.
Siehst du eines dieser Symbole in deinem Workbook, findest du in der App …

- alle **Audios**
- alle **Videos** und **Erklärfilme**
- **Hilfen** und **Lösungen** zu ausgewählten Aufgaben

Cornelsen

Titelbild
Cornelsen/Tauziehen Bild re.: Anja Poehlmann, Häuschen Bild li.: Shutterstock.com/JoolsW

Illustrationen
Cornelsen/Harald Ardeias: (S. 8 1-6; S. 9 1-8; S. 10 oben re.; S. 19; S. 23 mitte re.; S. 24 1-4; S. 27 oben re.; S. 31 A-H; S. 37-38; S. 39 1-4; S. 40 mitte re.; S. 42 oben re.; S. 45 A-C; S. 46 A-H; S. 47; S. 53 A-C; S. 60 unten re.; S. 62 1-9; S. 64 oben re.; S. 68 unten re.; S. 74 oben re.; S. 75 oben re.; S. 83 oben); **Cornelsen/Irina Zinner**: (S. 1 Möwe; S. 5 Möwe; S. 10 Möwe; S. 11 Möwe; S. 18 Möwe; S. 25 Möwe; S. 40 Möwe; S. 66-67 Möwen; S. 81-82 Möwen; S. 88 Möwen).

Abbildungen
Umschlaginnenseite vorne (U2): siehe unter S. 8, S. 9, S. 80; **S. 5** 1-5: Cornelsen/Anja Poehlmann; **S. 6**: Cornelsen/Anja Poehlmann; **S. 7** oben re.: Cornelsen/Anja Poehlmann; **S. 8** mitte li.: Shutterstock.com/Peredniankina; **S. 10** unten re.: stock.adobe.com/@CPPHOTOGRAPHIC/Chris; **S. 11** oben re.: mauritius images/Pitopia, unten re.: stock.adobe.com/Andrey Lapshin; **S. 12** mitte re.: stock.adobe.com/zefart; **S. 13** oben re.: Cornelsen/Anja Poehlmann; **S. 15** mitte re.: Shutterstock.com/Amorn Suriyan; **S. 20** oben li.: Shutterstock.com/Peredniankina, mitte re.: mauritius images/Pitopia; **S. 23** 1: stock.adobe.com/iiierlok_xolms**,** 2: stock.adobe.com/TALVA, 3: stock.adobe.com/designer_an; 4: stock.adobe.com/iiierlok_xolms; **S. 26** 1: stock.adobe.com/Peredniankina, 2: Shutterstock.com/Max Topchii, 3: Shutterstock.com/Erika Cross, 4: Shutterstock.com/ANURAK PONGPATIMET; **S. 30** oben re.: akg-images/DN/TT News Agency; **S. 33** 1: stock.adobe.com/Marina Lohrbach, 2: stock.adobe.com/cynoclub,3: stock.adobe.com/Kathrin39, 4: Shutterstock.com/Kapitula Olga, 5: Shutterstock.com/photobeps, 6: stock.adobe.com/baibaz. 7: Shutterstock.com/Stocksnapper, 8: Shutterstock.com/Ko Backpacko, 9: Shutterstock.com/ozanuysal; unten re.: stock.adobe.com/tgordievskaya; **S. 35** mitte re.: akg-images/TT NEWS AGENCY; **S. 39** unten: Shutterstock.com/Noch; **S. 41** A: stock.adobe.com/Pavel Losevsky, B: Shutterstock.com/Rittis, C: Shutterstock.com/fotoknips, D: stock.adobe.com/matimix, E: stock.adobe.com/Mary, F: Shutterstock.com/Pazargic Liviu; **S. 44** mitte: Shutterstock.com/Monkey Business Images, 1: mauritius images/Science Source, 2: stock.adobe.com/nahhan; **S. 46** 4: stock.adobe.com/Brocreative, 5: Shutterstock.com/PhotoRoman, 6: stock.adobe.com/Mary, 7: stock.adobe.com/Pictures/EKH/EKH-Pictures; **S. 50** oben li.: stock.adobe.com/WONG SZE FEI, mitte li.: Shutterstock.com/szefei; **S. 52** unten: Shutterstock.com/Monkey Business Images; **S. 54** 1-4: Shutterstock.com/Azizah's; **S. 56** A: stock.adobe.com/Gino Santa Maria, B: stock.adobe.com/Paul Lawrenson 2017/Paul, C: stock.adobe.com/weyo, D: stock.adobe.com/jessicagirvan, E: stock.adobe.com/aamulya, F: stock.adobe.com/Copyright 2019 Ruth Black; **S. 57** A: stock.adobe.com/Mara Zemgaliete, B: stock.adobe.com/emilio100, C: stock.adobe.com/monstersparrow, D: Shutterstock.com/G.MARTYSHEVA, E: Shutterstock.com/masa44, F: Shutterstock.com/a_v_d, G: stock.adobe.com/ozmen, H: stock.adobe.com/VectorBum, (unten) 1: stock.adobe.com/VALERIA TARLEVA/valery121283, 2: stock.adobe.com/volff, 3: stock.adobe.com/praha.cz/etienne@vosk/Moving Moment, 4: Shutterstock.com/azure1, 5: stock.adobe.com/karandaev, 6: stock.adobe.com/Nataliia Pyzhova; **S. 58** 1: stock.adobe.com/Irina, 2: Shutterstock.com/CKP1001, 3: Shutterstock.com/vm2002; **S. 59** mitte li.: Shutterstock.com/ANURAK PONGPATIMET, unten re.: mauritius images/Pitopia; **S. 65** 1+8: stock.adobe.com/moonkin, 2: stock.adobe.com/VectorBum, 3+6+9: stock.adobe.com/MicroOne; 4+5: stock.adobe.com/Stalvalki, 7: stock.adobe.com/macrovector; **S. 68** mitte re.: mauritius images/Pitopia; **S. 70** 1-4: Shutterstock.com/Teguh Mujiono, 5-6: stock.adobe.com/inspiring.team, unten li.: Shutterstock.com/mavo; **S. 75** mitte re.: Shutterstock.com/Chrispictures; **S. 76** unten li.+re.: Shutterstock.com/LemonadePixel, unten mi.: stock.adobe.com/Tartila; **S. 77** unten re.: stock.adobe.com/a4stockphotos; **S. 79** mitte re.: stock.adobe.com/AS Photo Family; **S. 80** mitte re.: Cornelsen/Grasshopper Films LTD; **S. 85** mitte re.: stock.adobe.com/AS Photo Family; **S. 86** mitte re.: stock.adobe.com/zefart; **S. 87** (oben) 1: Shutterstock.com/Perutskyi Petro, 2: stock.adobe.com/VectorBum, 3: stock.adobe.com/Baiba Opule/baibaz, 4: Shutterstock.com/Svetlana Serebryakova, 5: stock.adobe.com/karandaev, 6: stock.adobe.com/Pictures/EKH/EKH-Pictures, (mitte) 1+3: Shutterstock.com/LemonadePixel, 2: Shutterstock.com/VikiVector;

Hello again!
The last day of the holidays

1 Our four friends

▶ SB, p. 11

a) **Look at the messages on pages 10 and 11 in your book and then complete the sentences below.**

1 Lily and Zane — 'We don't want ______ to go back to school.'

2 Noah — 'I like ______ school.'

3 Sunita — 'What do ______ you think ______?'

b) **Complete the questions and short answers with *do / don't / does / doesn't*.**

4 Do ______ Lily and Zane want to go back to school? – No, they don't ______.

5 Does ______ Noah like school? – Yes, he does ______.

6 Does ______ Noah have his old bag? – No, he doesn't ______.

I, you, we, they **do**
he, she, it **does**

c) **Write the question and the short answer.**

7 Sunita / want / a new pencil case? – Yes.

Does Sunita want a new pencil case ______? – Yes, she does ______.

2 Sunita and Noah

▶ SB, p. 11

Look at Sunita's and Noah's messages on page 11 in your book. Then complete the sentences with the correct words from the box.

has • he's (x2) • her (x3) • his • is • ~~likes~~ • she's • they're

Noah (1) likes ______ school. (2) He's ______ at home. (3) He's ______ wearing (4) his ______ new school uniform. He (5) has ______ a new school bag too.

Sunita (6) is ______ in town with (7) her ______ mum. (8) They're ______ buying (9) her ______ last school things. (10) She's ______ looking for a new pencil case. She can't wait to see all (11) her ______ friends at school.

3 Back to school

► SB, p. 11

Match the words and phrases from the box with the verbs 1–10. You don't need two phrases from the box.

a day on the beach • delicious • your eyes • feel sad • happy to be at school • homework • late • on the beach • a picture • see my friends • tomorrow • a uniform

1 wear *a uniform*

2 do *homework*

3 enjoy *a day on the beach*

4 taste *delicious*

5 can't wait to *see my friends*

6 hang out *on the beach*

7 draw *a picture*

8 close *your eyes*

9 sleep *late*

4 School words

► SB, p. 11

Complete the mind map with as many school words as you can. You can work with a partner.

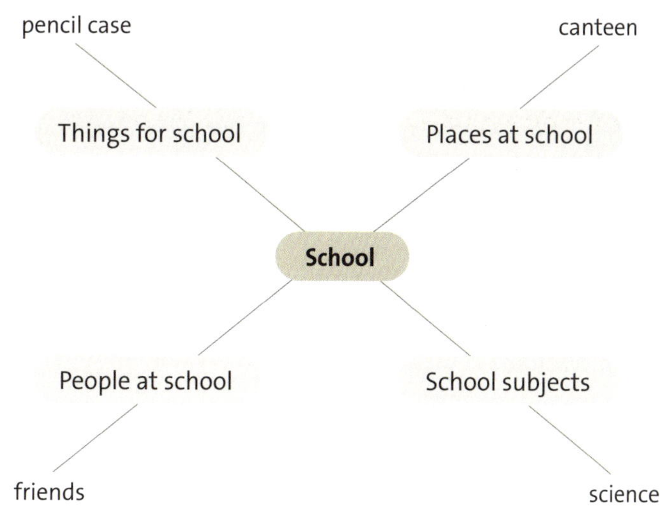

Unit 1
Travel and holidays

1 On holiday

►SB, p. 13

Where can you be on holiday? Look at pages 12 and 13 in your book and write the correct words.

in the *mountains*

on a *campsite*

in a *holiday* apartment

at my *aunt's* house

near an amazing *beach*

in *France*

2 READING Oscar's holidays

►More help, p. 20 ►SB, p. 13

Read about Oscar's holidays. Then answer the questions.

At the end of July I was at my grandma's house in Watford. It was a great week with two day trips to London. I was lucky, because it was sunny all week. In August I was in Spain for two weeks with my mum, dad, my sister Olivia and my brother Freddie. We were in a nice big hotel. We weren't next to the sea, but we were near the sea. My dad likes the sea, but my mum likes the mountains, so some days we were on the beach, and some days in the mountains. It was hot near the sea, but windy and a bit cold in the mountains.

1 When was Oscar in Watford? *At the end of July / In July.*

2 Why was Oscar lucky? *Because it was sunny (all week).*

3 Where was Oscar for two weeks in August? *In Spain.*

4 Where was their hotel? *Near the sea.*

5 What was the weather like on the beach? *Hot.*

I can talk about my holidays and the weather.

Erklär-film

3 LANGUAGE Simple past: positive Oscar's holiday in Spain

► SB p. 14

Write a sentence for each picture.

We	listened stayed sunbathed watched had swam were went	amazing ice cream. dancers in the street. in the sea. on a campsite. on the beach. to flamenco music. to Spain. very happy there.

1  *We went to Spain.*

2  *We stayed on a campsite.*

3  *We swam in the sea.*

4  *We sunbathed on the beach.*

5  *We had amazing ice cream.*

6  *We listened to flamenco music.*

7  *We watched dancers in the street.*

8  *We were very happy there.*

4 LANGUAGE Simple past: positive My holiday at home last year

► SB, p. 15

Write the ten regular verbs in the simple past.

> !
> Regular verbs in the simple past:
> (verb) + ed
> (verb ends in e) + d

I (1) *stayed* (stay) at home in the holidays last year and it wasn't boring! I love cycling so I (2) *cycled* (cycle) every day. I (3) *listened* (listen) to some of my favourite podcasts. I (4) *started* (start) to play the guitar, and I (5) *practised* (practise) every day. Well, most days. OK, some days. But I also (6) *helped* (help) mum a bit at home. I (7) *cooked* (cook) some meals and I sometimes (8) *remembered* (remember) to put out the rubbish! I (9) *loved* (love) playing with our cat and I (10) *looked after* (look after) the goldfish. Holidays? I was really busy!!

01

5 LISTENING A scary holiday story

► SB, p. 16

a) Ling tells you about her holiday in Whitby, a town in the north of England. Listen to her and tick (✓) the correct sentence A–D.

Always read the sentences before you listen!

1 Ling was in Whitby, in the north of England,

- A many years ago. [ ]
- B last summer. [ ]
- C last winter. [✓]
- D in April this year. [ ]

2 Ling and her family were

- A in a hostel. [ ]
- B in a hotel. [ ]
- C in a holiday apartment. [✓]
- D on a campsite. [ ]

3 In Whitby

- A Ling's family were the only tourists. [ ]
- B there were many other visitors. [✓]
- C there were no tourists in the shops. [ ]
- D there were some other visitors, but not many. [ ]

4 Ling knows the story of Dracula because

- A she watched the film. [✓]
- B she listened to a podcast. [ ]
- C her teacher told the story in class. [ ]
- D she has the book. [ ]

5 In the story, Dracula was a vampire

- A in Germany. [ ]
- B in Russia. [ ]
- C twenty years ago. [ ]
- D a long time ago. [✓]

6 Now Ling

- A wants to watch the film again. [ ]
- B is too scared to watch the film again. [ ]
- C wants to get the book. [✓]
- D wants to buy a Dracula costume. [ ]

b) Read sentences 1–6 and then listen again. Are the sentences true (T), false (F) or not in the text (NT)?

1	Whitby is always really dark.	F
2	Ling likes scary movies.	NT
3	Dracula the vampire travelled to England.	T
4	In Whitby, Dracula was a woman.	F
5	The guide wore a Dracula costume.	NT
6	The guide told Ling more about Dracula.	T

6 LANGUAGE Simple past: positive A holiday in Italy

▶ More help, p. 20 ▶ SB, p. 17

a) Write the simple past form of the verbs.

You can find the verbs on pages 14, 15 and 16 in your book.

	simple past:		simple past:
do	did	take	took
go	went	tell	told
have	had	think	thought
swim	swam	wear	wore

Italy

b) Now complete the text with the correct verbs from a).

In my holiday last year I (1) went to Italy with my family. We (2) did a lot of exciting things there. Usually I get up late, but there I (3) swam in the sea every day before breakfast. It was hot and sunny, so I (4) wore a summer hat. The woman at the hotel (5) told us where to buy the best food! I (6) took a lot of photos, and we all (7) had a really good time. We all (8) thought Italy was great, and we would like to go again next year!

7 LANGUAGE Simple past: positive Oscar's holiday in October

▶ SB, p. 17

a) Read the text and look at the verbs in blue.

Circle the regular verbs and underline the irregular verbs.

Regular verbs have simple past forms with -ed. But irregular verbs have special forms!

In my week's holiday I (1) stayed (stay) at home. Some days I (2) played (play) with my brother and sister and we (3) watched (watch) some films together. We (4) had (have) good fun. My mum and dad (5) worked (work) on most days, but we (6) did (do) something together on Friday: we all (7) went (go) to a show in London. The music (8) was (be) great, and the people (9) wore (wear) amazing costumes! I really (10) enjoyed (enjoy) it.

b) Now write the correct forms of the verbs in the simple past.

I can write about my holiday activities. ✓

02–05

8 LISTENING Times

▶ Digital help ▶ SB, p. 18

- Choose five times: 9.15 9.50 10.08 10.18 11.14 11.40 12.20 1.12 1.32 2.10 2.59.
  Write them in the boxes.
- Play the game in groups. Listen. When you hear your times, cross them out (~~9.15~~).
- If you hear all five times, shout "Here!". The game ends – you win!

Game 1

Game 2

Game 3

Game 4

9 LISTENING AND SPEAKING Train times

▶ SB, p. 19

a) Partner B: Look at page 86.

Partner A: Listen to Partner B. Write the times of the trains.

Train to Brighton: 14.13

Train to Hastings: 14.21

Train to Eastbourne: 14.03

Train to Portsmouth: 14.09

b) The train to Brighton is late. Ask your partner about it and write the information.

Excuse me, please. When is the next train to Brighton?

new arrival time is 14.45

new platform: 1

c) Look at the information and read the train station announcements[1].

The next train to Woking is at 19.05 at platform 3. Platform 3 for the 19.05 train to Woking.

The next train to ... is at ... at platform ... Platform ... for the ... train to ...

The next train ...

Woking 19.05	Platform 3
Gatwick Airport 18.48	Platform 1
Epsom 18.59	Platform 11
Dorking 19.12	Platform 8
(For Dorking change in Redhill.)	

d) Look at the information in c) and answer your partner's question.

e) Now check your answers with your partner.

[1] **announcement** *Ansage*

Erklärfilm

10 LANGUAGE Simple past: negative Brighton Pride

▸ SB, p. 20

a) **Look again at the text on page 20 in your book.**

What's true? Circle the correct answer.

Lily (1) **went** / **(didn't go)** with her mum and dad. She (2) **(went)** / **didn't go** with her friends. Sunita (3) **(bought)** / **didn't buy** a Pride flag. Lily (4) **bought something** / **(didn't buy anything)**. Noah (5) **(wore)** / **didn't wear** headphones. Lily and her friends (6) **(watched)** / **didn't watch** the people in the parade, but they (7) **talked** / **(didn't talk)** to their friend Willow and her girlfriend. They (8) **(ate)** / **didn't eat** rainbow cake in the Family Pride area. After the parade they (9) **(listened)** / **didn't listen** to street musicians, but (10) **went** / **(didn't go)** to the concert.

b) **Check your answers with a partner. Then check your answers together in the book.**

11 LANGUAGE Simple past: negative Ling and Oscar's weekends

▸ SB, p. 20

a) **Read the sentences about Ling. Write the infinitive form of the verbs 3–10.**

b) **Oscar didn't do what Ling did. Complete the sentences 2–10 about Oscar in the simple past.**

Ling	Verb	Oscar
1 Ling did her homework.	do	1 Oscar didn't do his homework.
2 She texted her friends.	text	2 He didn't text his friends.
3 She ate some cake.	eat	3 He didn't eat cake.
4 She listened to music.	listen	4 He didn't listen to music.
5 She went into town.	go	5 He didn't go into town.
6 She saw a friend in town.	see	6 He didn't see a friend in town.
7 She bought a present.	buy	7 He didn't buy a present.
8 She visited her aunt.	visit	8 He didn't visit his aunt.
9 She put on Pride make-up.	put	9 He didn't put on make-up.
10 She had a great time.	have	10 He didn't have a great time.

12 Words in Unit 1

▶ More help, p. 21 ▶ SB, p. 20

Write the words in the puzzle.

1 When you travel by train you must have a ...

2 One tooth, two ...

3 You see with this.

4 In the Pride Parade some people wear a special ...

5 a pet 6 1000

7 A ghost tour goes ... the dark parts of a town.

8 You ... somebody when you put your hand on them.

9 This is what something costs.

10 One foot, two ...

11 In the UK, the ... is pounds (£) and pence (p).

12 This is where the train arrives in a train station.

13 One child, two ...

13 LANGUAGE Simple past Your weekend

▶ Digital help ▶ SB, p. 21

a) **Write three things you did, and three things you didn't do last weekend!**

I went shopping with ... I didn't ...

____

____

____

____

____

b) WALK AROUND **You have four minutes. How many partners can you find with at least three sentences like your sentences?**

I went to the cinema.

Me too! I went to the cinema too!

And I had popcorn.

Ah, sorry! I didn't have popcorn!

▶ Early finisher 1, p. 19

I can talk about a special day in my holidays.

14 READING Oscar's idea

▸ SB, p. 23

Read Oscar's article and sentences 1–6. Are the sentences true (T) or false (F)?

1 The woman from 'Keep Britain Tidy' talked to Oscar and his friends in his home. *F*
2 Oscar first thought 'What this woman says is false'. *T*
3 Oscar and his friends bought their equipment from a place in town. *F*
4 There were a lot of plastic bags in the rubbish. *T*
5 Oscar thinks picking rubbish was a good experience. *T*
6 Oscar says that people think too much about rubbish. *F*

www.schoolpaper.example.com

My big idea – *by Oscar*

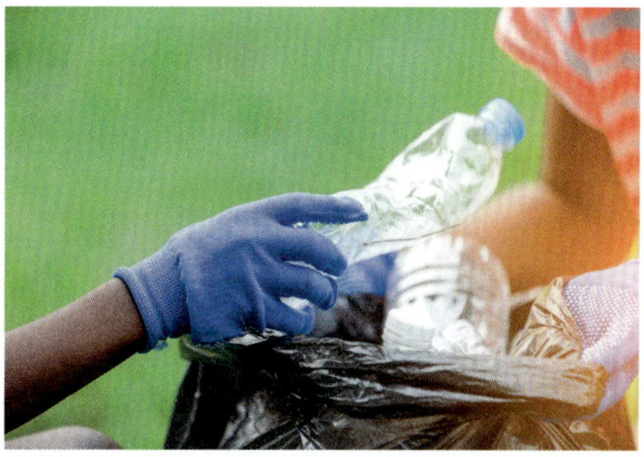

About six months ago a woman from a group called 'Keep[1] Britain Tidy' came and talked to us in assembly about the problem of rubbish. She told us that people drop[2] two million pieces of rubbish in Britain every day, in towns, next to roads, on the beaches, etc. 'Don't accept[3] rubbish in the streets!' was her message.

Two million pieces? I didn't think she was right. So after school I looked online, and saw that yes, she was right. 'That's terrible,' I thought. 'What can I do?'

The field next to our school is a place where people stop and have picnics. And there is always a lot of rubbish in the field – pieces of paper, bottles, pieces of plastic, and things like that. So some friends and I made a plan and we told other students about it. We borrowed rubbish-pickers from a place in town, we bought some big black plastic bags and one Saturday morning we all went to the field. We put on our gloves and began to pick rubbish.

I was surprised to find so much rubbish and so many plastic bags. I thought people didn't use plastic bags any more. And I was angry. I thought, 'With so much rubbish everywhere, places like this field aren't safe for animals and children. That's terrible!' We had different bags for plastic bottles, for cans[4] and for the rest of the rubbish. And when we stopped we had ten bags in all. Then we had a picnic in the field. We ate sandwiches, fruit, chocolate, and more and of course we put all the paper and plastic in our bags!

Last weekend there was a ceremony and our little group got a prize. I was proud of what we did, but I am still angry. Why is there so much rubbish everywhere? Don't people see it? Or don't they think when they drop a can or a plastic bottle? How can people be so stupid?

Source: https://www.keepbritaintidy.org/faqs/advice/litter-and-law#:~:text=More%20than%20two%20million%20pieces,look%20untidy%20and%20uncared%20for (31.01.2023)

▸ Challenge 1, p. 21

[1] **keep** *(be)halten* [2] **drop** *fallen lassen* [3] **accept** *akzeptieren* [4] **can** *Dose*

I can **talk about last weekend.**

15 READING What is the story about?

▶SB, pp. 24–26

Look at the story on pages 24–25 in your book. Texts A, B, C are all true. Tick (✓) the one that tells the story best.

A
It's about Noah's first train journey alone and about all the nice things he did when he was with Buddy and his grandma in Portsmouth. ☐

B
It's about how Noah, after a nice day in Portsmouth, was alone in a scary situation. But he did the right thing, his friends helped him and he felt good in the end. ☑

C
It's about how travelling by train can be difficult because it is so easy to get on the wrong train. And then you are in real trouble. ☐

16 READING How? What? Who? Why?

▶SB, pp. 24–26

Answer the questions about Noah's adventure.

1 How often does Noah usually see his grandma in Portsmouth? *Once a month.*

2 What did Noah do in Portsmouth with his grandma? *They went to the beach, had a picnic.*

3 Why did Noah take the wrong train? *The station was loud and he was tired.*

4 What did Noah do then? *He hugged Buddy and texted his friends.*

5 How did Noah's friends help him? *They helped him find the right train to Brighton.*

17 Language in the story

▶Digital help ▶SB, pp. 24–26

Write the opposites. The words are in Noah's story.

1 into Brighton – *out of Brighton*

2 with other people – *alone*

3 difficult – *easy*

4 at first – *in the end*

5 fast – *slow*

6 the right train – *the wrong train*

7 opened my eyes – *closed my eyes*

8 horrible – *nice*

☒ 18 What do you think?

▶Digital help ▶SB, pp. 24–26

Complete the sentences. You can use words from the box for the first part of the sentences.

brave • helpful • kind • mean • stupid • ...

1 I think Noah was *(brave)* because *(he travelled alone by train)*.

2 I think Noah's friends were *(kind)* because *(they helped him)*.

I can talk about new experiences.

19 Funny plural forms (not just -s)

Write the plural forms of these words.

1 foot *feet* 2 woman *women* 3 fish *fish*

4 tooth *teeth* 5 man *men* 6 knife *knives*

7 mouse *mice* 8 child *children* 9 shelf *shelves*

20 Word groups

a) **Write the words in the correct groups.**

b) **Write one more word in each list.**

angry • arrival • excited • ferry • plane • platform • return • taxi • tomorrow • two days ago • worried • yesterday

1 transport	2 When?	3 at the station	4 feelings
ferry	*tomorrow*	*arrival*	*angry*
plane	*two days ago*	*platform*	*excited*
taxi	*yesterday*	*return*	*worried*
(train)	*(next week)*	*(ticket)*	*(proud)*

21 SPEAKING Speak English well: The letter O

06 a) **Listen to the five words. How many different ways of saying the letter O do you hear?**

love hot do go brother 1 ☐ 2 ☐ 3 ☐ 4 ☑ 5 ☐

b) **Write the words in the correct groups.** ▸ Digital help

ago	another	bottle	concert	ghost	glove	hope
hospital	money	mother	move	only	oven	phone
podcast	shoe	told	two	who	wonderful	wrong

O as in love [ʌ]: *another, glove, money, mother, oven, wonderful*

O as in hot [ɒ]: *bottle, concert, hospital, podcast, wrong*

O as in do [uː]: *move, shoe, two, who*

O as in go [əʊ]: *ago, ghost, hope, only, phone, told*

07 c) **Listen and check your answers.**

08 d) **Listen again and repeat the words.**

e) **Write a (stupid) sentence with as many words from b) as you can!**

My favourite page in Unit 1 in my book:

My favourite page: (page 16) Why: (I like scary stories.)

Four words that are hard to say:

once
(mountain)
(exciting)
(through)

Four of the longest words:

announcement
(equipment)
(wonderful)
(underground)

I can:

Say what I did in the holidays: (I stayed at home, I cycled, I went into town, I sunbathed, I visited my aunt, ...)

Say what I didn't do at the weekend: I didn't buy anything, (I didn't go by plane, I didn't eat pizza, I didn't pick rubbish, ...)

I remember:

Ten regular verbs in the simple past: I played, practised, (listened, watched, looked, travelled, cycled, walked, stayed, talked)

Ten irregular verbs in the simple past: I saw, wore, (went, told, felt, came, thought, ate, got, bought)

How to say train times: I can say 8.15 ☐ 11.42 ☐ 12.25 ☐ 13.05 ☐ 16.59 ☐

Four useful questions at the station: Where is platform 3? (Can I pay by card? When is the next train to London? Do I need to change?)

My progress[1] in English:

☐ great!
☐ OK
☐ some things are quite difficult

Some things are difficult? You can ask your teacher or a friend for help!

[1] **progess** *Fortschritt*

Early finisher 1 Can you complete the ghost tour? ▶ Digital help

Start your ghost tour at START. There are ten ghosts. Each ghost makes you say five things.

- If you can say all five things, tick (✓) the box and you can move to the next ghost.
- If you can't, you can look at your book and find the answers.

Can you complete the ghost tour?

▶ Check

2 More help READING Oscar's holidays

▸WB, p. 8 ▸SB, p. 13

Read about Oscar's holidays. Then (circle) the correct answer.

At the end of July I was at my grandma's house in Watford. It was a great week with two day trips to London. I was lucky, because it was sunny all week. In August I was in Spain for two weeks with my mum, dad, my sister Olivia and my brother Freddie. We were in a nice big hotel. We weren't next to the sea, but we were near the sea. My dad likes the sea, but my mum likes the mountains, so some days we were on the beach, and some days in the mountains. It was hot near the sea, but windy and a bit cold in the mountains.

1 When was Oscar in Watford? A At the start of July. (B) At the end of July.

2 Why was Oscar lucky? A Because he was in London. (B) Because it was sunny.

3 Where was Oscar for two weeks in August? (A) In Spain. B In Watford.

4 Where was their hotel? A Next to the sea. (B) Near the sea.

5 What was the weather like on the beach? (A) Hot. B Windy and a bit cold.

6 More help LANGUAGE Simple past: positive A holiday in Italy

▸WB, p. 11 ▸SB, p. 17

a) **Write the simple past forms of the verbs. Choose the correct forms from the box.**

did • had • swam • thought • told • took • went • wore

	simple past:		simple past:
do	*did*	take	*took*
go	*went*	tell	*told*
have	*had*	think	*thought*
swim	*swam*	wear	*wore*

Italy

b) **Now complete the sentences with the correct verbs from a).**

In my holiday last year I (1) *went* (go) to Italy with my family. We (2) *did* (do) a lot of exciting things there. Usually I get up late, but there I (3) *swam* (swim) in the sea every day before breakfast. It was hot and sunny, so I (4) *wore* (wear) a summer hat. The woman at the hotel (5) *told* (tell) us where to buy the best food! I (6) *took* (take) a lot of photos, and we all (7) *had* (have) a really good time. We all (8) *thought* (think) Italy was great, and we would like to go again next year!

12 More help Words in Unit 1

▶ WB, p. 14 ▶ SB, p. 20

Write the words in the puzzle.

1 When you travel by train you must have a ...

2 One tooth, two ...

3 You see with this.

4 In the Pride Parade some people wear a special ...

5 a pet 6 1000

7 A ghost tour goes ... the dark parts of a town.

8 You ... somebody when you put your hand on them.

9 This is what something costs.

10 One foot, two ...

11 In the UK, the ... is pounds (£) and pence (p).

12 This is where the train arrives in a train station.

13 One child, two ...

								2		
		1	T	I	C	K	E	T		
		5			6		3	E	Y	E
	4	C	O	S	T	U	M	E		
		A			H			T		
	7	T	H	R	O	U	G	H		
	8				U					
	T		9		S		10			11
	O	12	P	L	A	T	F	O	R	M
	U		R		N		E			O
13	C	H	I	L	D	R	E	N		N
	H		C				T			E
			E							Y

Challenge 1 WRITING Oscar's idea

▶ WB, p. 15

Write a text to a friend about what Oscar did. Write 8–10 sentences.

I have a friend called Oscar. There's a field next to his ...
Oscar and his friends ...

Oscar wrote: My friends ...
But you write: Oscar's friends/His friends.

(I have a friend called Oscar. There's a field next to his school where people stop and have picnics. But there's always a lot of rubbish in the field. Oscar and his friends cleaned up this field with the help of other students. They borrowed equipment from a store in town and bought plastic bags. Together they collected ten bags of rubbish! They had different bags for plastic bottles, cans, and other rubbish. Oscar was very angry that there was that much rubbish. Then last week there was a ceremony and he and his friends won a prize for their clean-up.)

▶ Check

1 Verbs in the simple past

Erklär-film

a) Look at the verbs in blue in the text.
Verbs with simple past -ed → underline
Verbs with special forms → (circle)

> **!** In the simple past
> – some verbs end in -ed.
> – some verbs have special forms.

b) Now write the correct forms of the verbs in the simple past.

Last night I (1) stayed (stay) at home and (2) listened (listen) to music in my room. I also (3) did (do) my maths homework and then I (4) watched (watch) a film and (5) played (play) a game. After that I (6) went (go) to bed. It (7) was (be) cold in bed so I (8) wore (wear) my warm pyjamas!

2 More verbs in the simple past

Write the verbs in the simple past in the puzzle.

1 swim	7 put	13 hear	19 do
2 buy	8 begin	14 make	20 have
3 be *(we, you, they)*	9 go	15 eat	21 say
4 see	10 wear	16 get	
5 sleep	11 think	17 tell	
6 take	12 hang	18 ride	

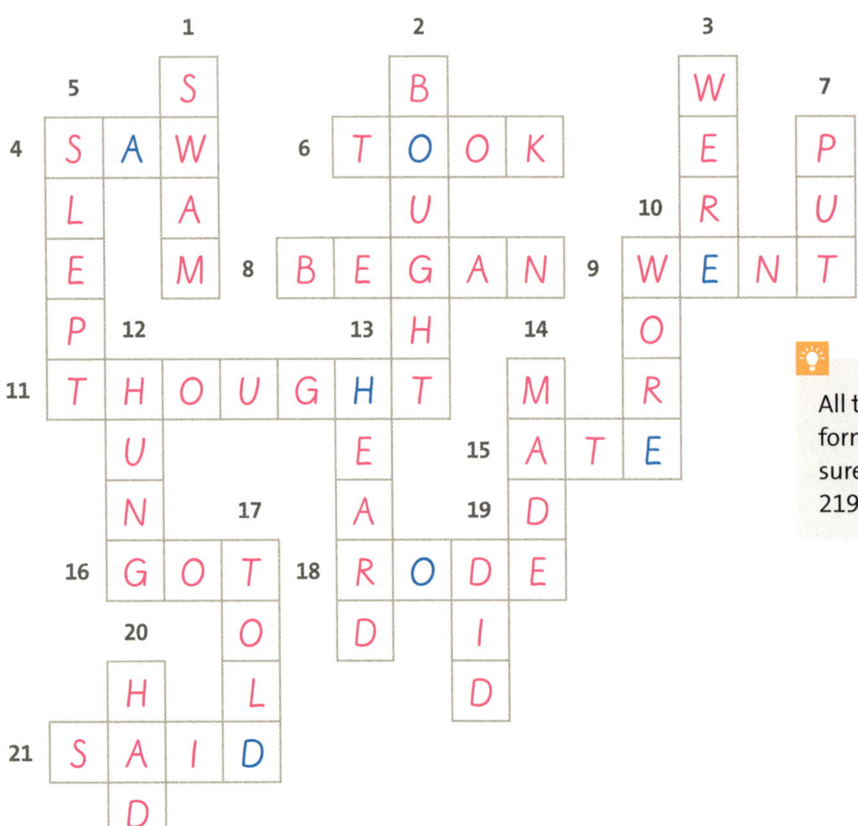

> All the verbs have special forms in the simple past. Not sure about them? Look at page 219 in your book.

▶ Check

Erklär-
film

3 Tia's family holiday

► Digital help

Tia's holiday went wrong. Write six negative sentences in the simple past.

1 We went to Italy by train. We *didn't go by plane.*

2 We stayed in a hotel. We *didn't stay on a campsite* .

3 We swam in the hotel pool. We *didn't swim in the sea* .

4 We had a lot of rain. We *didn't have a lot of sun* .

5 The holiday was OK. It *wasn't wonderful* .

6 The people in the hotel were OK. But they *weren't very friendly* .

!
Remember:
I saw
→ I didn't see
I played
→ I didn't play
I was
→ I wasn't
they were
→ they weren't

4 At the station

Tia helps a tourist at the station. Complete the dialogue with words from the box.

change • leaves • need • next • pay • platform • return • understand • welcome

Tia Hi. Do you (1) *need* help?

Tourist Yes, please, I do. I need a ticket to Manchester. But I don't (2) *understand* this ticket machine.

Tia No problem. Do you want a single or a (3) *return* ?

Tourist Just a single, please.

Tia Look, a single ticket to Manchester costs £27.50. Do you want to (4) *pay* by card?

Tourist Yes, I do. And when is the (5) *next* train to Manchester? Does the machine tell me that?

Tia Yes, it does. It (6) *leaves* in twenty minutes, from (7) *platform* 3.

Tourist Is it a direct train?

Tia No, it isn't. You need to (8) *change* in Birmingham.

Tourist Thank you so much!

Tia You're very (9) *welcome* . Bye!

► Check

Unit 2
Friends and heroes

1 LISTENING The head students in Varndean School

09

► SB, p. 42

Listen to Lily, Noah, Sunita and Zane. (Circle) the correct answer a or b.

1	Mihai is the head student for the four friends'	a class.	(b) house.
2	Noah knows Mihai because he spoke in	(a) assembly.	b an English lesson.
3	Sofia is the head student of	a Rackham House.	(b) Russell House.
4	Jodie, the head student of Angelou House, helped Finn	(a) last week.	b two weeks ago.
5	Faye is the head student of	(a) Ellis House.	b Attic House.

2 Describing people

► SB, p. 43

a) Match the descriptions and the pictures.

A This student has short hair. She doesn't have glasses, and she doesn't have braces. She's wearing a green sweatshirt. Picture 3	B This student is wearing a blue T-shirt. He has long curly black hair and looks friendly. He has brown eyes and he has glasses. Picture 2
C This student has blond hair and blue eyes. He has braces. He doesn't have glasses. Is he tall or small? I don't know! Picture 1	D This student has long straight hair. She's very tall. I think she's often funny. She doesn't have braces and she doesn't have glasses. Picture 4

1

2

3

4

b) And you? Describe yourself. Write as much as you can.

I have (green eyes and long straight brown hair. I have glasses.)

I don't have (braces or purple hair!)

I can describe what someone looks like.

3 What are people like?

▸ SB, p. 44

a) Look at the words in the box. Then read sentences 1–8 and complete the puzzle with eight words from the box. Cross out (~~cross out~~) the words that you use from the box.

brave • clever • confident • hard-working • helpful • kind • mean • patient • shy • strong • worried

1 She's like a boxer!

2 He's calm and always knows what to do.

3 She's top of the class in many subjects.

4 He does nice things for people.

5 She always has time to listen to other people when they talk about their problems.

6 He says what is right and true – even if other people laugh at him.

7 She always helps people when they need her.

8 He's not nice.

1					S	T	R	O	N	G		
2	C	O	N	F	I	D	E	N	T			
3						C	L	E	V	E	R	
4						K	I	N	D			
5						P	A	T	I	E	N	T
6							B	R	A	V	E	
7					H	E	L	P	F	U	L	
8						M	E	A	N			

b) Write the word in blue from a) under the correct definition A, B, C or D.

A She works a lot, at school and at home.	B When he says 'Yes', you know it means 'Yes'.	C She's quiet and not very confident when she meets new people.	D He's often not very happy because he thinks about problems.
hard-working	reliable	shy	worried

c) Now match the three words you didn't use in a) with the definitions in b).

Use the words from the box in a).

4 Listening Friends

10

▶ More help, p. 36 ▶ SB, p. 45

a) Alex interviews Oscar, his sister Olivia, his brother Freddie and Ling about their best friends. Listen to them and (circle) the two correct answers.

1 Oscar says Ling is

A confident.
(B) funny.
C hard-working.
(D) kind.

2 Freddie says his mum is

(A) happy.
B patient.
C brave.
(D) reliable.

3 Olivia says her friend Jessie is

(A) shy.
B strong.
(C) brave.
D confident.

4 Ling says Oscar is

A tidy.
(B) sometimes angry.
C sometimes mean.
(D) good fun.

b) Listen again and complete the sentences below with one or two words.

1 Oscar says that it's *important* to be kind.

2 Freddie says his mum makes him feel happy even when he isn't *really happy*.

3 Olivia says things like parkour are easy when you're *confident*.

4 Ling says that when they're together, she and Oscar have a *good time*.

▶ Early finisher 1, p. 35

5 Writing A really good friend

▶ SB, p. 45

Think of a really good friend – at school, in your family, in your street, etc. Write why you like this person so much. Write four sentences or ☒ six sentences.

Ideas: *I love my mum! She's always ...*

My best friend is not always ..., but I like him because ...

You can use words from exercises 3 and 4.

(My best friend is Tina. She isn't always reliable because she's sometimes late. But she's always very helpful. She's never mean and we have a good time together. She's very brave when we watch scary movies together. I really like her!)

I can describe my friend's personality.

Erklär-film

6 LANGUAGE Simple past: *yes/no*-questions and short answers

▸ SB, p. 49

Look at the picture of Oscar's day out. Then answer the questions.

Yes,	he	did.
No,	she	didn't.
	they	

1 Did Oscar go to the mountains?
– No, he didn't.

2 Did he wear a hat?
– No, he didn't.

3 Did he take a bottle of water?
– Yes, he did.

4 Did Oscar go with his brother Freddie? – No, he didn't.

5 Did Ling eat an apple? – No, she didn't.

6 Did Oscar and Ling have a good time? – Yes, they did.

7 LANGUAGE Did Oscar and Ling do the same things?

▸ More help, p. 36 ▸ SB, p. 49

a) **Read the sentences 1–4. Complete the questions.**

> ! I stay**ed** → Did you stay? No **-ed** in the question!

1 Oscar listened to music. Did Ling listen to music? – No, she didn't.

2 He played some games. Did Ling play games? – Yes, she did.

3 He visited a friend. Did Ling visit a friend? – Yes, she did.

4 He texted his dad. Did Ling text her dad? – Yes, she did.

b) **Now read sentences 5–9 and complete the questions.**

> ! Here the form of the verb changes. I **saw** → Did you **see**?

5 Ling went into the sea. Did Oscar go into the sea? – No, he didn't.

6 She swam in the sea. Did Oscar swim in the sea? – No, he didn't.

7 She bought an ice cream. Did Oscar buy an ice cream? – Yes, he did.

8 She told a scary story. Did Oscar tell Ling a scary story? – Yes, he did.

9 She left at about six o'clock. Did Oscar leave at about six o'clock? – Yes, he did.

Erklär-film

8 LANGUAGE Simple past: questions with question words All about you ► SB, p. 49

a) Write the questions with the words in the correct order.

b) Now answer the questions in full sentences.

1 *to bed / when / you / did / go / last night / ?*

When did you go to bed last night?

– I went to bed last night at (9 p.m.)

2 *you / to bed / go / why / did / at that time / ?*

Why did you go to bed at that time?

– I went to bed then because (I was tired.)

3 *for breakfast / you / did / what / this morning / have / ?*

What did you have for breakfast this morning?

– I (had pancakes for breakfast.)

4 *did / how / to school / come / you / ?*

How did you come to school?

– I (came to school by bike.)

5 *your first lesson / you / have / where / did / ?*

Where did you have your first lesson?

– I (had P.E. in the sports hall.)

9 LANGUAGE Win or lose? ► Digital help ► More help, p. 37 ► SB, p. 49

a) Write five questions about last weekend which you think your partner will answer with 'No, I didn't.'.

1 Last weekend, did you (see an elephant)? ☐

2 Did you (buy a bike)? ☐

3 (Did you go to London)? ☐

4 (Did you visit Scout)? ☐

5 (Did you play football with a dog)? ☐

b) Now ask your partner your questions and your partner answers.
Tick (✓) the box for 'Yes, I did.' and put an ✗ in the box for 'No, I didn't.'.

c) Now answer your partner's questions. The partner with more ✗ wins.

10 Language Mum's many questions

▸ Digital help ▸ SB, p. 49

When Oscar came home from town, his mum wanted to know ... everything!
Read the dialogue and write his mum's questions.

Mum Why did you go to town, Oscar?
Oscar I met somebody.
Mum Who did you meet?
Oscar I met Ling. We went to the cinema.
Mum Oh, what film did you watch?
Oscar We watched *Superhero III*. Then we went for a walk.
Mum Where did you go?
Oscar To the park. And we ate something.
Mum What did you eat?
Oscar Some pizza. And then we came home.
Mum How did you come home?
Oscar By bus.
Mum Why did you take the bus? You can walk!
Oscar Oh, Mum! I was tired!

11 Reading A hero for today

▸ SB, p. 51

a) **Read Oscar's article on the next page. Then read the questions and answer with short answers.**

1 Did Greta Thunberg save a baby from the sea? No, she didn't.
2 Did she sit inside an important building? No, she didn't.
3 Did a lot of people sit with her on the first day? No, they didn't.
4 Did she talk to people the next day? Yes, she did.
5 Did lots of people hear her message? Yes, they did.

b) **What about you? Do you think Oscar's hero is a great hero?**
Complete one of the sentences.

1 Yes, because (14 million people took action to save the planet. / she tried to save the world. / ...)

2 No, because (it was many years ago. / there aren't many protests today. / people don't know her today. / ...)

www.schoolpaper.example.com

My hero – *by Oscar*

My hero is a girl, and she was famous[1] around the world when she was only 15. What did she do? She didn't do anything exciting or dramatic. She didn't run into the sea and save a baby from the water. She just sat[2] in front of an important building in a capital city. She didn't scream or make a loud noise. But it was a Friday, and she didn't go to school.

And she spent that difficult first day all alone. I think that's very brave. I don't like being all alone for three or four hours!

But the next day some people asked the girl why she was there. And she said she was there to save our planet. It was a strong message, because it was easy to understand. And many people thought, 'Do you know what? She's right!' And soon students in countries around the world went to demonstrations on Fridays and said. 'We must do more for our planet.' In 2019, an amazing number of people took action[3] to save the world – 14 million! And many more people heard her message in the media.

There are still protests today. Everybody remembers the picture of Greta Thunberg sitting alone. Everybody remembers her message. And everybody knows her message is still true.

▸ Early finisher 2, p. 35

12 Techno quiz

▸ SB, p. 52

a) **Work with a partner.**

Partner A reads out the three dates in answers 1, 3, 5.
Partner B reads out the three dates in answers 2, 4, 6.

1 When was the world's first computer?	1832	✓	1852	☐	1932	☐
2 When were there one million computers in the world for the first time?	1980	✓	2000	☐	2010	☐
3 When was the first video film from Mars?	1995	☐	2010	☐	2021	✓
4 When was the world's first message by internet?	1949	☐	1969	✓	1999	☐
5 When was the world's first mobile phone with a camera?	1975	☐	2000	✓	2010	☐
6 When was the world's first smartphone?	1994	✓	2004	☐	2014	☐

b) **Read the questions and discuss the answers with your partner. Tick (✓) the correct date.**

11 c) LISTENING **Now listen to the answers. Were you right in part b)?**

[1] **famous** *berühmt* [2] **sit (simple past: sat)** *sitzen* [3] **take action** *aktiv werden*

I can **ask and answer questions about my hero.**

13 Clothes for superheroes

▸ SB, p. 53

Look at the letters 1–8 and pictures A–H. Write the words and match the pictures.

1 t o b o s — boots [E]

2 o s s h e — shoes [A]

3 c p e a — cape [D]

4 s r d e s — dress [C]

5 e t e m l h — helmet [H]

6 m i w t s s i u — swimsuit [B]

7 u o r e s r s t — trousers [G]

8 k m s a — mask [F]

A

B
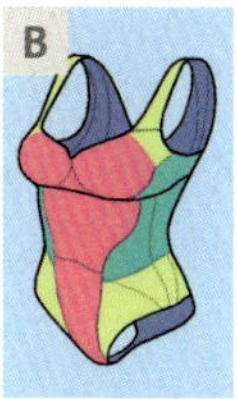
C

D
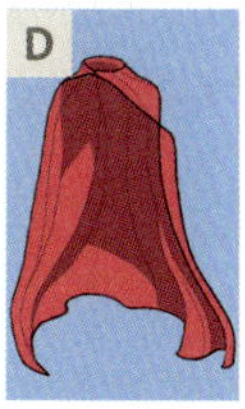
E
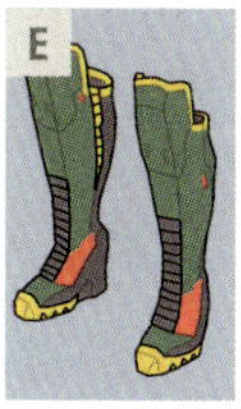
F

G

H

14 LANGUAGE Subordinate clauses with conjunctions
The day I needed a superhero

▸ SB, p. 53

a) **Complete the sentences with the correct endings from the box.**

> I became really scared • it became windy • my family lived in France • when I hurt my leg • we often went to the mountains

1 When I was born, my family lived in France.

2 When we were in France, we often went to the mountains.

3 But once we climbed a mountain when it became windy.

4 I knew we were in trouble when I hurt my leg.

5 And when dad said we were lost, I became really scared.

b) **Now write the second part of the sentence with the words in the correct order.**

6 When we knew we were lost, we all screamed. (screamed / we / all)

7 When we made a loud noise, some people heard us. (heard / us / some people)

8 I was so happy when they helped us. (when / they / us / helped)

They were real superheroes!

▸ Challenge 1, p. 37

I can write about superheroes.

15 READING Tell the story

► SB, pp. 54–56

Look at the story on pages 54–55 in your book. Answer the questions about the story.

1 What did the four friends and Finn talk about at the start of the story?

They talked about their free-time activities.

2 What do people do in parkour?

They jump from walls and climb things.

3 What was Finn's big mistake?

He tried parkour but he didn't have any practice.

4 How did the friends help Finn? Give six examples:

They called 999 / kept him warm / didn't let him fall asleep / stayed calm / did breathing exercises / got a blanket / told funny stories and jokes.

5 How did Finn's mum feel?

She *was upset.*

16 What do you think?

► SB, pp. 54–56

a) **Write what you think.**

1 Why do you think Finn wanted to do what Lily did?

(He thought it was easy. / He likes Lily. / ...)

2 Do you think the four friends did the right thing? Why (not)?

Yes, because *(they stayed calm. / they worked as a team. / ...)*

No, because *(Lily showed Finn parkour. / ...)*

b) **Compare your answers with a partner.**

17 LISTENING Verbs in the story

12

► SB, pp. 54–56

a) **Listen to the end of the story and write the missing verbs.**

1 The ankle doesn't *hurt* .

2 His head *seems* OK.

3 I can *take* you to his room.

4 I'm sorry that I *showed* you parkour.

5 Zane, can you *promise* me something?

6 Don't *tell* me any more jokes.

b) **Now listen again to the end of the story and check your answers.**

I can understand a story about teamwork.

18 Singular or plural?

Write the plural form of the words. Add -s or -es only if you must.

1 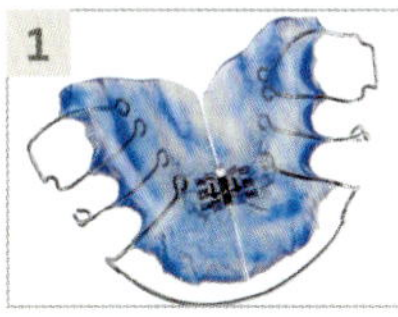
brace s

2 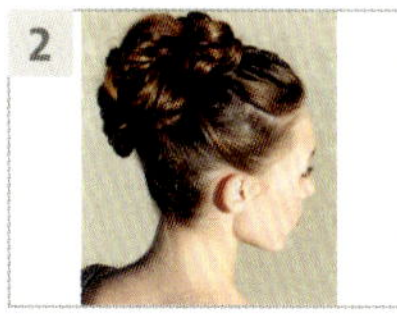
hair ___

3 
glass es

4 
trouser s

Are the words singular or plural in your language?

5 
vegetable s

6 
fruit ___

7 
rubbish ___

8 
clothe s

9 
headphone s

19 Small words

a) **Complete the sentences with the correct word from the box.**

ago • as • at • for • from • in • like • of • off • up

1 I often think of ___ my friend Aylin in Turkey.

2 We grew up ___ together in Turkey.

3 But I came here two years ago ___.

4 I'm happy when I get a text from ___ Aylin.

5 We often send messages in ___ the evening.

6 Aylin is good at ___ listening.

7 She has a job as ___ an influencer.

8 I want to be more like ___ her.

9 I can't wait for ___ July when I can see her again.

10 I'm so excited that I nearly fell off ___ my bike!

b) **Check your answers with a partner.**

20 Speak English well: Sandwich or language?

13
a) **Listen to the words. Can you hear how [tʃ] and [dʒ] are different?**

[tʃ] as in sandwich:	**[dʒ] as in language:**
cheese, teacher, children, chocolate, football match	joke, June, geography, fire engine, page

13
b) **Listen again and repeat the words in a).**

Jess is playing chess.

c) **Now say these sentences. Be careful with the sounds in blue.**

1 I like jelly!

2 Don't jump!

3 Did you enjoy your journey?

4 Are you German?

5 Are you vegetarian?

6 Did you start your new job in July?

My favourite pages in Unit 2 in my book: pages 52 and 53

Four words that are hard to write:

straight

(laugh) / (accident)

(trousers)

Useful question words:

Where? How?

What? When?

Why?

I can:

Say what people look like: (She has straight/curly hair, braces, glasses. / He is small/tall, ... / He's wearing jeans, ... / ...)

Describe a person's personality: (reliable, lazy, hard-working, good at sports, patient, strong, shy, confident, ...)

Ask and answer questions in the simple past: (What did you see? – We saw everything. / ...)

Say what a hero or superhero does: she helps people, (saves people from the sea, helps people when it's dangerous, ...)

I have learned:

Ten useful new verbs: spend, (marry, promise, climb, save, add, hang out with, fight, hit, was born, ...)

How to say dates: I can <u>say</u>: 2022 ☐ 2049 ☐ 1937 ☐ 1484 ☐ 2000 ☐

More parts of the body: face, (ears, nose, ankle, neck, leg, ...)

My progress in English:

Write 1–4 in the circles: 1 easy 2 quite easy 3 quite hard 4 hard

Speaking ◯ Writing ◯ Learning new words ◯

Write what you can do to get better: (Practise speaking at home more often. / ...)

Early finisher 1 Your perfect head student

a) Make a mind map with words and sentences that describe your perfect head student. Write as many ideas as you can.

My perfect head student

personality

clever

what they do

listen to all students

b) Compare with a partner. Did you have the same ideas?

▸ Check

Early finisher 2 Questions for Greta Thunberg

a) Read the text about Greta Thunberg on page 30 again. Then write some questions to interview her about her life as a child and about what she did in her protest. Use these ideas or your own.

Where / go / to school?
How / you / feel / when you ...?
Why / you / ...?

Where did you (go to school?)

(What are your hobbies?)

(Who is your hero?)

(How did you feel on the first day of your protest in 2018?)

(Why are the protests on Fridays?)

b) Compare your questions with your partner's questions. Choose the four best questions.

c) Now work with another pair and choose the four best questions for the interview.

▸ Check

4 More help LISTENING Friends

► WB, p. 26 ► SB p. 45

10

a) Alex interviews Oscar, his sister Olivia, his brother Freddie and Ling about their best friends. Listen to them and circle the two correct answers.

1 Oscar says Ling is	(A) funny.	B hard-working.	(C) kind.
2 Freddie says his mum is	(A) happy.	B patient.	(C) reliable.
3 Olivia says her friend Jessie is	(A) shy.	(B) brave.	C confident.
4 Ling says Oscar is	A tidy.	(B) sometimes angry.	(C) good fun.

b) Listen again and complete the sentences with one word.

1 Oscar says that it's *important* to be kind.

2 Freddie says his mum makes him feel happy even when he isn't really *happy*.

3 Olivia says things like parkour are easy when you're *confident*.

4 Ling says that when they're together, she and Oscar have a good *time*.

7 More help LANGUAGE Did Oscar and Ling do the same things?

► WB, p. 27 ► SB, p. 49

a) Read the sentences and write the verbs 2–4. Then complete the questions.

! I stay**ed** → Did you stay? No **-ed** in the question!

	Verb	Question
1 Oscar listened to music.	*listen*	1 Did Ling *listen* to music?
2 He played a game or two.	*play*	2 Did she *play* a game or two?
3 He visited a friend.	*visit*	3 Did she *visit* a friend?
4 He texted his dad.	*text*	4 Did she *text* her dad?

b) Now read these sentences and write the verbs 6–9. Then complete the questions.

! Here the form of the verb changes. I **saw** → Did you **see**?

	Verb	Question
5 Ling went into the sea.	*go*	5 Did Oscar *go* into the sea?
6 She swam in the sea.	*swim*	6 Did he *swim* in the sea?
7 She bought an ice cream.	*buy*	7 Did he *buy* an ice cream?
8 She told a scary story.	*tell*	8 Did he *tell* a scary story?
9 She left at about six o'clock.	*leave*	9 Did he *leave* at about six o'clock?

9 More help LANGUAGE Win or lose?

▶ Digital help ▶ WB, p. 28 ▶ SB, p. 49

a) **Write five questions about last weekend which you think your partner will answer with 'No, I didn't.'.**
Here are some ideas: *see an elephant? have a drink with …? swim underwater to …?*

1 Last weekend, did you (see an elephant) ______ ? ☐

2 Did you (buy a bike) ______ ? ☐

3 (Did you go to London) ______ ? ☐

4 (Did you visit Scout) ______ ? ☐

5 (Did you play football with a dog) ______ ? ☐

b) **Now ask your partner your questions and your partner answers.**
Tick (✓) the box for 'Yes, I did.' and put an ✕ in the box for 'No, I didn't.'.

c) **Now answer your partner's questions. The partner with more ✕ wins.**

Challenge 1 LANGUAGE Subordinate clauses with conjunctions
The day I needed a superhero

▶ Digital help ▶ WB, p. 31

Write about a day when something went very wrong and you needed help from a superhero.
Use ideas in the pictures or your own ideas.

1 When I was born, we lived in ______.

2 When we lived there, we often ______.

3 But once ______.

4 I knew ______ in trouble when ______.

5 And when ______, I felt scared.

6 When ______, some people ______.

7 I was so happy when ______.

1 Tia's friends

a) **Write about Tia's friends. Write the right words from the box.**

blond • braces • curly • eyes • glasses • straight • tall • worried

1 Sarah has *curly*  black hair and she wears *glasses* 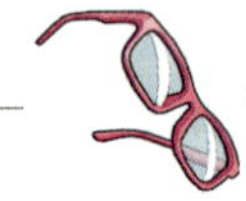.

2 Yuri is quite *tall* . He has *braces* 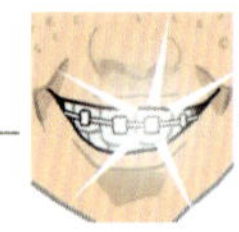.

3 Emily has *straight*  brown hair and brown *eyes* .

4 George has short *blond*  hair and often looks *worried* .

b) **Now complete the personality words with vowels (A E I O U) and Y.**

1 Sarah isn't sh*y*. She's str*o*ng and c*o*nf*i*d*e*nt, but sometimes l*a*z*y*.

2 Yuri is h*a*rd-w*o*rk*i*ng, p*a*t*i**e*nt and r*e*l*i**a*bl*e*. And he's g*o**o*d at sport.

3 Emily is k*i*nd, h*a*pp*y* and often very f*u*nn*y*. I think she's br*a*v*e* too.

4 George is cl*e*v*e*r and h*e*lpf*u*l. He's sometimes *a*ngr*y* but he's never m*e**a*n.

2 A holiday in Spain

Erklär-film

Match the questions and answers about a holiday. Write letters A–H below.

1 *C* 2 *E* 3 *H* 4 *G* 5 *D* 6 *A* 7 *F* 8 *B*

1 Where did you go on holiday?
2 Why did you go there?
3 How did you go there?
4 Where did you stay?
5 What did you do there?
6 Did you have a good time?
7 When did you come back?
8 Was the plane late?

A Yes, we did.
B No, it wasn't.
C We went to Spain.
D We went swimming and we visited our friends.
E Because we have friends there.
F Last week.
G In a holiday apartment.
H We went by plane.

► Check

3 Questions, questions, questions

Complete Uncle Tim's boring questions and Tia's short answers: ✓ = yes, ✗ = no.

1 Did you have breakfast this morning, Tia? Yes, I did. ✓

2 Did your parents go to work early? No, they didn't. ✗

3 Did your brother get up late? No, he didn't. ✗

4 Did your mum take/drive you to school? Yes, she did. ✓

5 Was school hard today? No, it wasn't. ✗

6 Were your friends happy to see you? Yes, they were. ✓

7 Was the food in the cantine good? Yes, it was. ✓

4 Clothes and things

What are the models wearing? And what do they have? Write the words.

1

blue sweatshirt

useful bag

nice trousers

2

cool glasses

great swimsuit

beach blanket

3

cycling gloves

strong helmet

black boots

4

summer hat

long dress

dancing shoes

5 Body words

What hurts? Write the words.

1 my neck	2 my ankle	3 my legs
4 my head	5 my ear	6 my foot

▸ Check

Unit 3
Activities and games

1 Activities in Brighton

▶ SB, p. 73

Write the missing words. They all have the letters EA in them.

1 There's a panto at the th EA tre in Brighton.
2 It's called B EA uty *and the Beast*.
3 You must be in your s EA ts by quarter past two.
4 You can l EA rn to cook Thai food.
5 That is a very cr EA tive activity.
6 You must be at l EA st 1.3 m for the zip challenge.

You can find the words on pages 72 and 73 in your book.

2 A times quiz

▶ SB, p. 73

Read the sentences and write the times. Use *quarter* and *half*, and write the times in words.

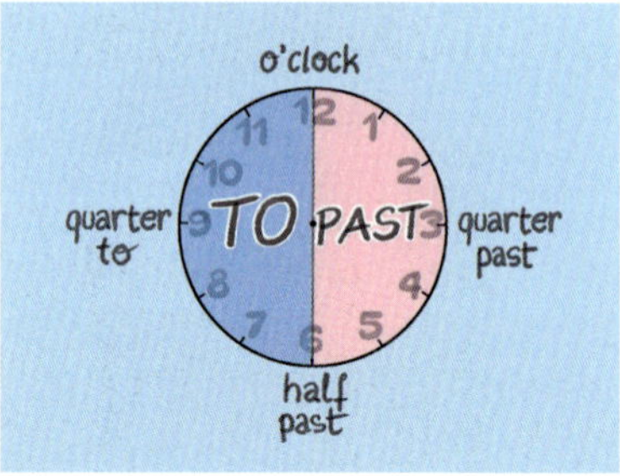

1 I arrived in Brighton 30 minutes ago, at 10.00 a.m.
What's the time now? It's half past ten.
2 We're in our seats, 15 minutes before the show begins at 7.00.
What's the time now? It's quarter to seven.
3 I want to meet my friend Hamid at 2.45. That's in 30 minutes.
What's the time now? It's quarter past two.
4 My sister went to the Family Arts Centre at four o'clock. That was 45 minutes ago.
What's the time now? It's quarter to five.

3 Crazy things to book

▶ SB, p. 73

a) **What crazy activities would you like to book? Write two crazy ideas.**

1 I'd like to book ______
2 I'd like to book ______

b) **Read your ideas in class. Who has the best idea?**

I can say what time activities start and end.

4 Amberley Museum

▸ SB, p. 74

Amberley Museum is about one hour from Brighton. Write the verbs.

> The verbs are on page 74 in your book.

(1) V i s i t Amberley Museum. (2) D i s c o v e r our old trains and buses. (3) P r a c t i s e riding an old bike! (4) T r y the delicious food in our cafe. (5) P r e p a r e at home for your visit with our online puzzles. (6) F i n d o u t when we're open on our website.

5 LISTENING Plans for Saturday

14

▸ SB, p. 75

a) **What are the people going to do on Saturday? Listen to Oscar, and write the letter of the correct picture under the people.**

Mum	Freddie and Olivia	Me (Oscar!)	My cousin Amelia	Grandma and Grandpa	All of us!
C	F	D	B	E	A

b) **Read questions 1–6. Then listen again and answer the questions.**

1 At what time is Mum going to leave the house? at half past nine

2 Who are Freddie and Olivia going to go out with? some friends

3 What is Oscar preparing for? a competition

4 When is Amelia's course? in the afternoon

5 When are Grandma and Grandpa going to be at Oscar's house? at half past five

6 How does Oscar feel about what they're going to do in the evening? excited

Erklär-film

6 LANGUAGE Going to-future Plans for the holidays

▶ SB, p. 76

a) Oscar and some of his friends at school are planning to go away in the holidays.
In each sentence
1. write the correct form of *be* in the box.
2. write the rest of the sentence with the words in the correct order.

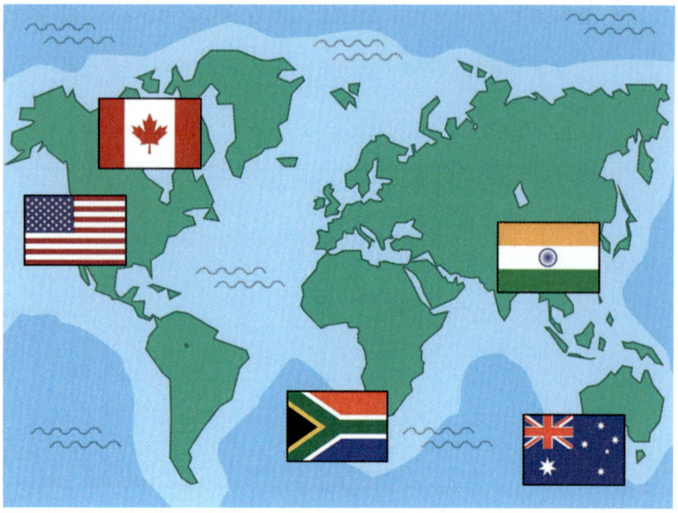

1 Ravi and Aara [are] going to stay with their aunt in India.
stay / going / to / in India. / with their aunt

2 Ling [is] going to go on a road trip in South Africa.
in South Africa. / going / on a road trip / to / go

3 Yuki and Akio [are] going to see the Niagara Falls in Canada.
in Canada. / going / the Niagara Falls / to / see

4 Jim [is] going to to relax on a beach in Australia.
in Australia. / going / on a beach / to / relax

5 And I ['m] going to visit my cousins in the United States.
in the United States. / visit / to / going / my cousins

6 So we ['re] all going to be in English-speaking countries.
in English-speaking countries. / going / be / to

b) **What are the people not going to do? Complete the sentences with the negative form of *going to*.**

1 Ravi and Aara aren't going to go to Mumbai. It's too busy.
2 Ling isn't going to ride on elephants. It's bad for the animals.
3 Yuki and Akio aren't going to visit Vancouver. It's too far away.
4 Jim isn't going to forget his sun hat. The sun is very strong over there.
5 I'm not going to see a show in New York. It's too expensive.
6 We aren't going to speak German for a few days.

Erklär-film

7 LANGUAGE Going to-future: yes/no questions Not fair

▶ SB, p. 77

Match the questions and answers. Write A–F in the boxes.

1 Are we going to have chips for dinner, Dad?
2 Is mum going to have dinner with us?
3 And what are we going to do after dinner?
4 Are Freddie and Olivia going to watch too?
5 Oh! What are you going to watch?
6 That's not fair! What am I going to do?

A Olivia's favourite film.
B You're going to do your homework, Oscar!
C No, we aren't. We're going to have pasta.
D Well, I'm going to watch a film.
E No, she's going to be home late.
F Yes, they are. They're going to watch with me.

1	2	3	4	5	6
C	E	D	F	A	B

8 LANGUAGE Going to-future: yes/no questions Freddie's questions

▶ SB, p. 77

a) **Read Oscar's answers. Then write Freddie's questions.**

▶ More help, p. 52

Freddie What *are you going to do* after school, Oscar?

Oscar After school? I'm going to go to town.

Freddie *Is Ling going to go with you* ?

Oscar No, Ling isn't going to go with me. I'm going to go with Amina and Karl.

Freddie Where *are you going to go* in town?

Oscar We're going to go to the theatre.

Freddie Oh, lucky you. *What are you going to see*, Oscar?

Oscar We're going to see the panto.

b) WRITING **And you? Write two things that you're going to do tomorrow. And two things that you're not going to do.**

____

____

____

____

▶ Early finisher 1, p. 51

I can make plans and talk about them. ✓

9 Talking about music

► SB, p. 78

a) Underline the adjectives that describe music.

tall relaxing calm curly quiet fast yellow slow weird loud

b) What sort of music do you like?

I like (pop music. / rap music. / rock music. / ...)

10 Language Comparatives Talking about hobbies

Erklär-film

► More help, p. 52 ► SB, p. 79

Write the adjectives in the comparative form.

I love knitting. It's (1) more relaxing (relaxing) than games. And it's (2) more creative (creative). I knit when I feel sad, and then I feel (3) happier (happy).

Yes, but dancing is (4) more energetic (energetic). OK, it's (5) louder (loud), but it's (6) cooler (cool) and (7) more exciting (exciting) too.

I'm not good with my hands, so for me drawing is hard. And knitting is (8) worse (bad). Photography is (9) better (good). It's much (10) easier (easy) than knitting!

► Challenge 1, p. 53

11 Language Comparatives What can you see?

► Digital help ► SB, p. 79

Read the sentences. Circle the correct word *than* or *as* and then tick (✓) the correct sentence.

1 In diagram 1

- A is longer than / as B. ☐
- A is as long than / as B. ☑
- B is longer than / as A. ☐

2 In diagram 2

- table A is as big than / as table B. ☑
- table A is bigger than / as table B. ☐
- table B is bigger than / as table A. ☐

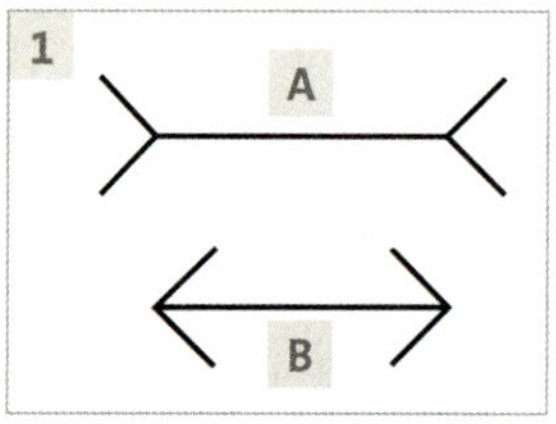

12 LANGUAGE Superlatives

Erklär-film

▸ More help, p. 53 ▸ SB, p. 81

a) **Complete the questions with the adjectives in the superlative form.**

A

The small car, 1990

B

The sports car, 2016

C

The big family car, 2021

1 Is the sports car the *cheapest* (cheap) car? – No, it *isn't.*

2 Which is the *most expensive* (expensive) car? – *The big family car.*

3 Is the small car the *oldest* (old) car? – *Yes, it is.*

4 Is the sports car the *newest* (new) car? – *No, it isn't.*

5 Which do you think is the *fastest* (fast) car? – *The sports car.*

6 Which do you think is the *best* (good) car? – *(The small car.)*

b) **Now look at the pictures and answer the questions in a).**

▸ Early finisher 2, p. 51

13 A mind map about films

▸ SB, p. 81

Complete the mind map with words from the box.

action • aliens • amazing music • an accident • doctors • dragons • exciting • great actors • love • popular • sad • scary • space • special effects • sportspeople • terrible • the life of a dancer • war

The main characters are: *aliens, doctors, dragons, sportspeople*

Topics in films: *an accident, love, space, the life of a dancer, war*

films

The film is *exciting, popular, sad, scary, terrible*

The film has *amazing music, action, great actors, special effects*

I can **compare music, shows and films.**

14 Places in town

▸ SB, p. 83

a) Read the sentences and look at the pictures. Then write the correct eight words in the puzzle.

1 A place where you can see a pantomime.
2 This is where trains stop.
3 A place with lots and lots of trees.
8 A place where you can borrow books.

4 
5 
6 
7 

1					T	H	E	A	T	R	E	
2	S	T	A	T	I	O	N					
3		F	O	R	E	S	T					
4				Z	I	P	W	I	R	E		
5				B	R	I	D	G	E			
6			C	A	S	T	L	E				
7			S	Q	U	A	R	E				
8						L	I	B	R	A	R	Y

b) Write a definition for the place in blue.

It's the place where you must go if *you're (very) ill / not well.*

15 Directions

▸ SB, p. 83

Match the phrases and the pictures.

1 Go through the forest.
2 Turn left.
3 Go straight on.
4 Go past some shops.
5 Turn right.
6 Go across the bridge.
7 Go up the street.
8 Go down the street.

1	2	3	4
C	H	A	F
5	6	7	8
D	G	B	E

A 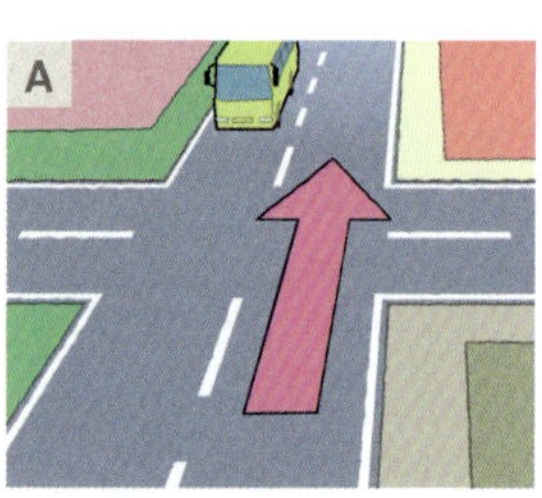
B 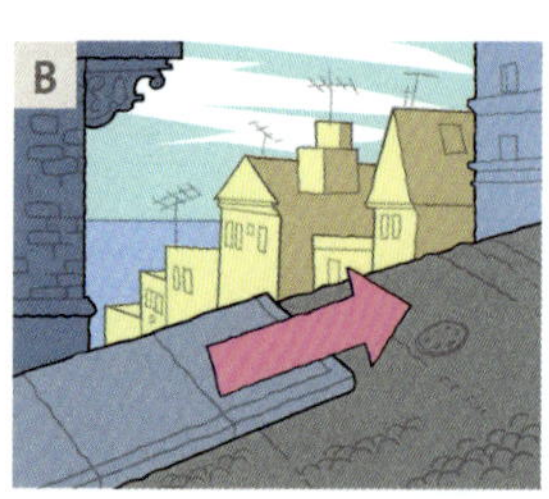
C 
D 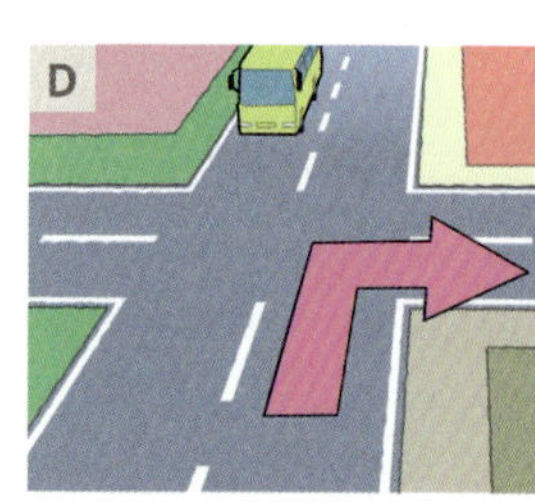
E 
F 

G 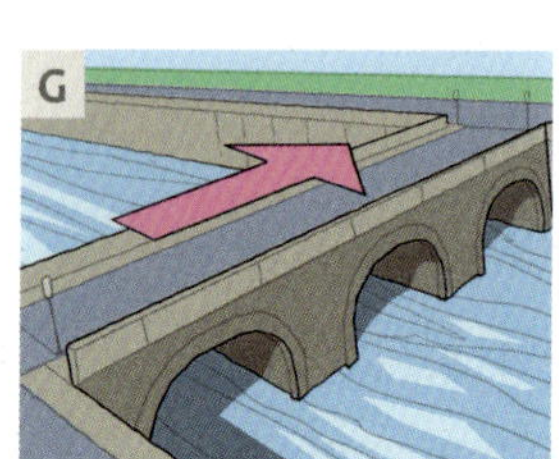
H 

16 In town

▶ SB, p. 83

15

a) LISTENING **Listen to the directions. Where do the directions take you to?**

1 *shopping centre* 2 *King's Square* 3 *zip wire* 4 *hospital*

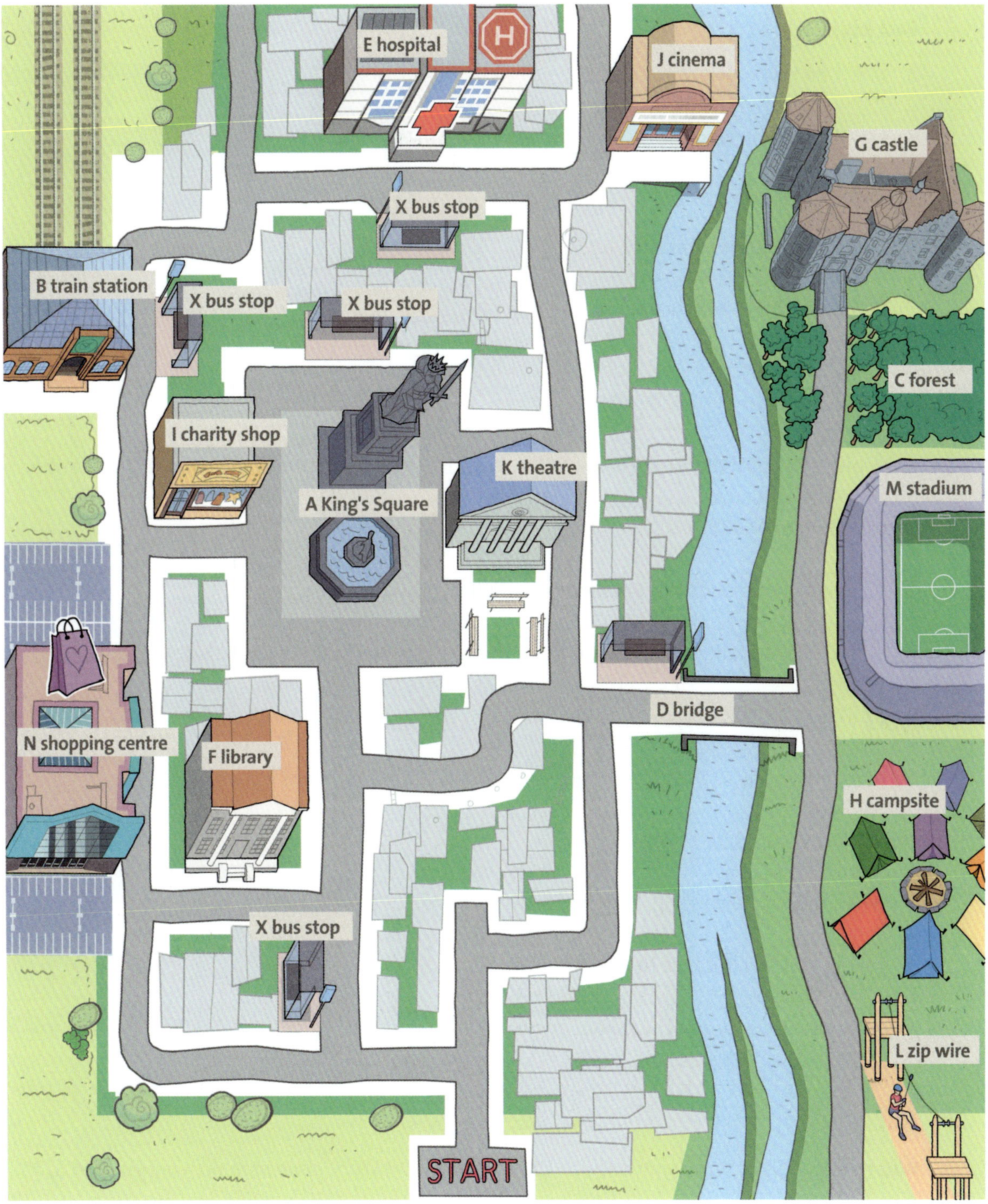

b) SPEAKING **Work with a partner.**

- Give your partner directions to a place in town but don't say which place it is.
- Your partner listens and follows on the map. Does your partner arrive at the correct place?
- Then swap roles.

I can **understand and give directions.**

17 VIEWING What's the missing word?

▸ SB, p. 87

Watch the video and write the missing words.

Part 1 (00:30 to 01:11)

1 Joe: 'Come with me after school tomorrow! And I can teach you some new *things*.'

Part 2 (01:12 to 01:37)

2 Joe: 'Don't worry, we'll go *slow*.'

3 Joe: 'The person who dances well and learns the most will *win*.'

Part 3 and 4 (01:38 to 05:08)

4 Joe: 'That's OK, Emir. Let's try *again*.'

5 Gloria: 'That was so much fun. Let's do some *more*!'

18 VIEWING Wrong information

▸ SB, p. 87

a) **Cross out (~~cross out~~) the wrong information in each sentence and write the correct information.**

Part 1 (00:30 to 01:11)

1 Daisy asks her friends to do gardening with her ~~this evening~~. *this week*

2 Gloria doesn't want to do gardening because she has ~~Maths Club~~. *photograpy club*

Part 2 (01:12 to 01:37)

3 When they meet at the street dance club, ~~Emir~~ teaches the others how to dance. *Joe*

Parts 3 and 4 (01:38 to 05:08)

4 When they begin dancing, Emir finds it really ~~easy~~. *hard*

5 Emir is a winner because he ~~danced~~ the most. *learned*

b) **Now watch the video, and check your answers with a partner.**

19 And you?

▸ SB, p. 87

What do you think? Write your answer. Useful words: *fun, scary, good at it, do what you like, ...*

Do you like freestyle dancing? Why (not)?

I (don't) like freestyle dancing

because ______________________.

20 Words in Unit 3

Write the words in the puzzle. You can work with a partner.

1 In a house, use the ... to go up.
2 Where the sun, moon and planets are.
3 Someone from a different planet.
4 These tell you how to play a game.
5 The places where you sit in a theatre or cinema.
6 You have this when your head hurts.
7 You use it to take photos.
8 Don't turn left, don't turn right, go ... *(2 words)*.
9 very, very bad
10 In a place, but I don't know where!
11 In a cinema, the film is on a big ...
12 Like a newspaper, but with longer articles and more colour photos.
13 A farm animal.
14 When you are next to things on two sides, you are ... them.

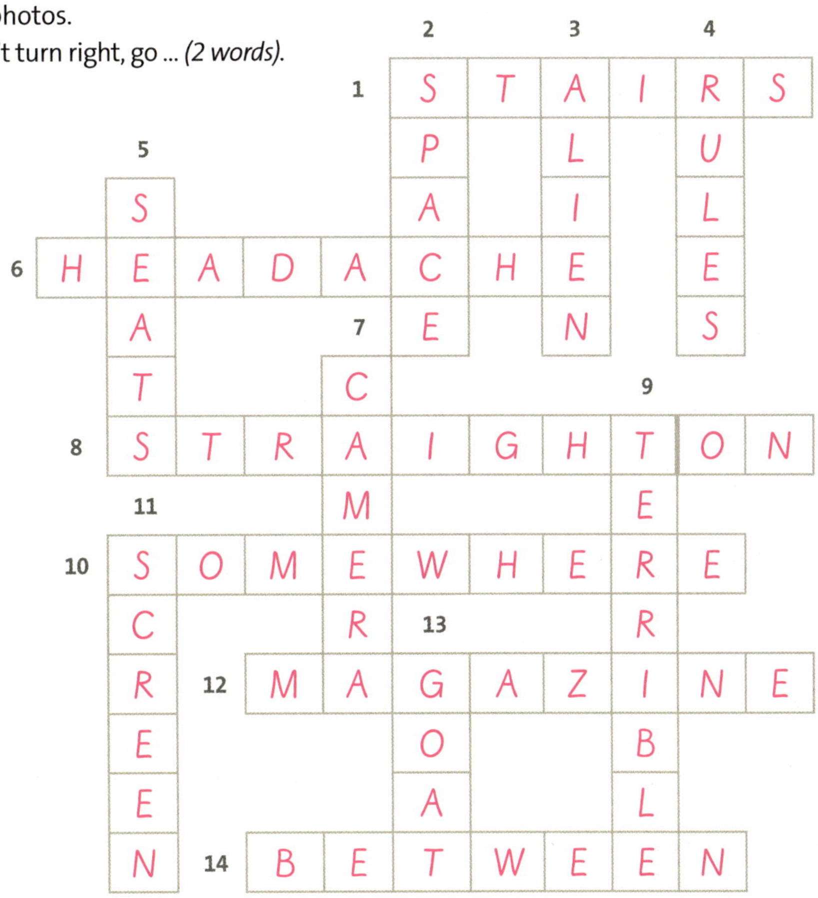

21 SPEAKING Speak English well: How do you say EA?

a) How do you say EA in the words in the box? Write them in the correct pronunciation[1] categories.

beach • break • ~~bread~~ • dead • ~~great~~ • head • healthy • ~~meal~~ • mean • meat • season • weather

1 [iː] meal, beach, meat, mean, season

2 [eɪ] great, break

3 [e] bread, dead, head, healthy, weather

16 **b) Now listen to the words. Were your answers in part a) right?**

[1] **pronunciation** *Aussprache*

My favourite topic in Unit 3 in my book: ______

Different kinds of music:

rap, (rock,
acoustic, classical, ...)

What I know about British pantomimes:

great shows, (funny, musical,
songs, the audience sings and talks
to the actors, funny costumes)

I can:

Tell the time:  It's quarter past three.

 It's half past six.

 It's quarter to eleven.

Make plans for the weekend: I'm going to (visit my aunt. We're going to go shopping. / ...)

I can use the comparative und superlative forms of adjectives:

tall: I am taller / the tallest

exciting: This film is more exciting / the most exciting.

good: I think electro music is better / the best.

bad: (This song) is worse / the worst.

Give directions: Turn (right/left. Go straight on. Go across the bridge. / ...)

My progress[1] in English:

What's easy or difficult when I write English?

Write 1–4 in the boxes: 1 easy 2 quite easy 3 quite hard 4 hard

having good ideas ☐ thinking of the right word ☐ spelling ☐ grammar ☐

[1] **progress** *Fortschritt*

Early finisher 1 Your plan for a perfect Saturday

a) READING Read Oscar's plan for a perfect Saturday.

> In the morning *I'm going to stay in bed till half past ten.*
> For lunch *I'm going to have sausages, eggs and chips.*
> After lunch *I'm going to play football with my friends.*
> *And then we're going to eat jelly and custard in the park!*
> In the evening *I'm going to go to a show at the theatre.*

b) WRITING Now write a plan for your perfect Saturday. What are you going to do?

In the morning *I'm going to* ____________________

For lunch ____________________

After lunch ____________________

____

In the evening ____________________

c) Compare your plan with a partner. What ideas are the same? What ideas are different?

Early finisher 2 Quiz questions

a) Use the internet and find the answers to these questions about Britain.

1 What's the highest mountain in Britain? *Ben Nevis*

2 What's the longest wall in Britain? *Hadrian's Wall*

3 How long is Severn, the longest river in Britain? *354 km*

4 How old is the oldest tree in Britain? *2000/3000 years old*

5 What is the tallest building in Britain? *The Shard*

▸ Check

b) Now write two quiz questions for your partner. Can your partner find the answers?

What's the highest / longest / oldest / biggest ... in ...?

____________________?

____________________?

8 More help LANGUAGE Freddie's questions

▸ WB, p. 43 ▸ SB, p. 77

a) **Read Oscar's answers. Then write Freddie's questions.**

Freddie What are you going to do after school, Oscar?

Oscar After school? I'm going to go to town.

Freddie Is Ling going to go with you?

Oscar No, Ling isn't going to go with me. I'm going to go with Amina and Karl.

Freddie Where are you going to go in town?

Oscar We're going to go to the theatre.

Freddie Oh, lucky you. What are you going to see, Oscar?

Oscar We're going to see the panto.

10 More help LANGUAGE Comparatives Talking about hobbies

▸ WB, p. 44 ▸ SB, p. 79

a) **Write each adjective in the box in the correct category.**

bad • cool • creative • easy • energetic • exciting • good • happy • loud • relaxing

Ends in y: easy, happy

Short adjective: cool, loud

Long adjective: creative, energetic, exciting, relaxing

Has a special comparative form: bad, good

b) **Write the adjectives in the comparative form.**

I love knitting. It's (1) more relaxing (relaxing) than games. And it's (2) more creative (creative). I knit when I feel sad, and then I feel (3) happier (happy).

Yes, but dancing is (4) more energetic (energetic). OK, it's (5) louder (loud), but it's (6) cooler (cool) and (7) more exciting (exciting) too.

I'm not good with my hands, so for me drawing is hard. And knitting is (8) worse (bad). Photography is (9) better (good). It's much (10) easier (easy) than knitting!

Challenge 1 WRITING **Talking about hobbies**

▸ Digital help ▸ WB, p. 44

Write about three hobbies or activities. Give your opinion with the comparative form of the adjectives. Use some of the words below or your own ideas.

cheaper than, more popular than, funnier than, more exciting than, ...

Example: I think parkour is more exciting than football.

___

___

___

___

___

12 More help LANGUAGE **Superlatives**

Erklärfilm

▸ WB, p. 45 ▸ SB, p. 81

a) **Write the adjectives in the superlative form.**

Short adjectives: cheap – cheapest

Long adjectives: expensive – most expensive

Has a special superlative form: good – best

b) **Complete the questions with the adjectives in the superlative form.**

The small car, 1990

The sports car, 2016

The big family car, 2021

1 Is the sports car the cheapest (cheap) car? – No, it isn't.

2 Which is the most expensive (expensive) car? – The big family car.

3 Is the small car the oldest (old) car? – Yes, it is.

4 Is the sports car the newest (new) car? – No, it isn't.

5 Which do you think is the fastest (fast) car? – The sports car.

6 Which do you think is the best (good) car? – (The small car.)

c) **Now look at the pictures and answer the questions in b).**

1 The time

What time is it? Write the times in words, not numbers.

1 02:00 2 05:15 3 08:30 4 10:45

1 It's *two o'clock.*

2 It's *quarter past five.*

3 It's *half past eight.*

4 It's *quarter to eleven.*

2 No school tomorrow

Erklär-film

Write the sentences with *going to*.

Remember:

I'm	I'm not	going to
She's	She isn't	
They're	They aren't	

Olivia *I'm not going to be* at school tomorrow. (I / not / be)

Karim Oh? What *are you going to do*? (you / do)

Olivia *Ms Jones is going to take* us to a museum in York. (Ms Jones / take)

Karim Oh, sounds cool. *Are you going to be* there all day? (you / be)

Olivia I think so. *We're going to have* lunch in a park. (we / have) And *we aren't going to be* back in time for the last lesson. (we / not / be)

3 New words in Unit 3

a) Write the words.

1 Twelve pages, each page with one month of the year. A *c a l e n d a r*

2 The words of a song. The *l y r i c s*

3 The points at the end of a football match, for example: 3–1. The *s c o r e*

4 The part of your phone or laptop that shows you the information. The *s c r e e n*

5 How you feel when you're not interested in things. You feel *b o r e d*.

6 The people who sit and watch in a theatre. The *a u d i e n c e*

7 The opposite of the top. The *b o t t o m*

b) Use the letters in yellow and write the word.

A film that you make by drawing lots of pictures is a *cartoon.*

▸ Check

Erklär-film

4 Which show?

▸ Digital help

a) Tia and her friends Seb and Kim are talking about three shows. Write the blue adjectives in the comparative or the superlative form. Write *the* or *than* if you need to.

The Star Cinema is showing
THE BLUE FOREST
'The best film of the year!'
£8.50

— FAMILY PANTO —
CINDERELLA
at the
Grand Theatre
£12.99

Live concert
Best
DANCE MUSIC
from Ireland
In the City Hall
£15 – £35

Tia I think the film looks (1) more interesting than (interesting) the panto.

Kim Really? I like funny things, and the panto is (2) funnier than (funny) the film.

Seb I think the concert is (3) the best (good) of all.

Tia Maybe, but the film is (4) cheaper than (cheap) the concert.

Kim Yes, that's true. The film is (5) the cheapest (cheap) of all three.

Tia And the concert is (6) the most expensive (expensive) of all!

Seb Yes, but a concert is (7) more relaxing than (relaxing) a panto.

Kim But a panto is more fun. Films are often (8) scarier than (scary) pantos.

Tia I don't agree. I think that films are (9) better than (good) pantos. Pantos are stupid. They are my (10) worst (bad) idea of an evening out!

Kim Well, OK then. Let's go to the film. Is that OK with you too, Seb?

Seb Fine with me.

b) **Now write the adjectives from part a) in the correct part of the table.**

1 comparative		
–er than	more ... than	*good* changes to:
funnier than	more interesting than	better than
cheaper than	more relaxing than	
scarier than		
2 superlative		
the -est	the most ...	*good* and *bad* change to:
the cheapest	the most expensive	the best
		the worst

▸ Check

Unit 4
Celebrate!

1 Pictures of celebrations

▶ SB, p. 103

a) **Look at the pictures A, B, C, D on pages 102 and 103 in your book.**
In which picture or pictures can you see 1–8? The answer can be one or more pictures.

1 masks D
2 vegetables A
3 lots of people B, C
4 nice things to eat A
5 colours at night C
6 two big eyes D
7 lots of colours A, B, D
8 things that make a loud noise C

b) **Write the correct words from the box under the pictures.**

A

fireworks

B

bonfire

C

candles

bonfire • candles • carnival • fireworks • food • presents

D

carnival

E

food

F

presents

▶ Early finisher 1, p. 67

2 One after the other

▶ More help, p. 68 ▶ SB, p. 103

Write out the blue words and information.

1 twenty, thirty, forty, fifty (30, 40, 50)
2 March, April, May, June (4th month, 5th month, 6th month)
3 spring, summer, autumn, winter (next three seasons)
4 six o'clock, quarter past six, half past six, quarter to eight (6.15, 6.30, 7.45)

I can **talk about celebrations.**

3 Things to eat and drink

▶ SB, p. 105

a) Look at the pictures. Complete the words with the letters A and/or E.

A

hon _e_ y

B

six _e_ g g s

C

_a_ p p l _e_ j u i c _e_

D

t _e_ _a_

E

t o m _a_ t o _e_ s

F

l _e_ m o n _a_ d _e_

G

c _a_ k _e_

H

c r _e_ _a_ m

b) Now complete the sentences with: *of* + the correct words from a).

1 Good morning. I'd like a bottle *of lemonade* and a pot *of cream*, please.

2 Hi, I'd like two cartons *of apple juice* and a packet *of tea*, please.

3 Hello. Do you have any jars *of honey*? And can I have one box *of eggs*, please?

4 I'd like three tins *of tomatoes*, please. Oh, and two pieces *of cake*, please.

4 A picnic with your partner

▶ SB, p. 106

a) Partner B: Look at page 87.
Partner A: Ask your partner if he/she has these things for a picnic. If yes, put a tick (✓). If no, put an ✗.

Do you have any ...?

eggs?	✓	yoghurt?	✗
strawberries?	✓	tomatoes?	✓
lemonade?	✗	salad?	✓

b) Now look at what you have.
Then listen to your partner and answer.

Yes, I do.

No, sorry, I don't.

✓

✓

✗

✗

✓

✓

c) Now write what you and your partner still need.

We still need *some ham, some cheese, some yoghurt and some lemonade.*

Erklär-film

5 LANGUAGE *some* and *any*, *a little* and *a few*

▶ SB, p. 107

a) **Read about Ling's breakfast, lunch and dinner. Write *some* or *any*.**

For breakfast I like to eat (1) some ____ toast with jam. I don't usually have (2) any ____ cereals, and I don't have (3) any ____ yoghurt. But on Sunday Dad makes breakfast and we have (4) some ____ eggs and (5) some ____ vegetarian sausages. I'm vegetarian, so I don't eat (6) any ____ meat. So for lunch I like to eat (7) some ____ salad or (8) some ____ rice with a nice curry. In the evening we have (9) some ____ baked beans on toast, or sometimes (10) some ____ pasta with a cheese sauce and (11) some ____ vegetables. But I don't have (12) any ____ tomatoes, because I don't like tomatoes.

b) **Now complete the recipes with *a little* and *a few*.**

1

2

3

1 For a carrot cake we need two eggs, a little ____ oil, a little ____ baking powder and a few ____ teaspoons of sugar. We also need a little ____ butter, a little ____ salt and of course a few ____ carrots!

2 For a trifle we need some cream, a little ____ custard, some jelly and a few ____ pieces of fruit.

3 For mattar paneer we need some tomato sauce, a few ____ peas and a little ____ pepper. We also need some bread and a few ____ vegetables.

▶ Early finisher 2, p. 67

6 LISTENING Four invitations to a meal

17

▶ SB, p. 107

Listen to four invitations. Write the missing information in the table.

	Time	Meal	Dessert
1	Friday 6.15	lamb ____ with potatoes and vegetables	ice cream
2	Monday 5.45	pasta with a tomato ____ sauce	fruit salad
3	Sunday 6.30	sausages with chips and baked beans	pancakes
4	Tuesday 5.30	vegetable soup ____ with bread and butter	cake

I can describe a special meal.

Erklär-film

7 LANGUAGE Present perfect Tired and happy

▶ SB, p. 109

Circle the correct form of *have* and the past particple.

1 Yasmin and Abdul are happy because they **has made / have made** a cake.

2 Fatima is tired because she **has practised / have practised** with her football team.

3 Jenny is happy because her parents **has come / have come** home.

4 Georgia is tired because she **has helped / have helped** a good friend.

5 And we're all tired because we **has worked / have worked** hard at school.

6 And me? I'm tired and happy because I **has finished / have finished** this exercise ☺.

8 LANGUAGE Present perfect Preparing for Oscar's birthday

▶ SB, p. 109

Complete the negative forms of the verbs in the present perfect: *hasn't* or *haven't*.

I (1) haven't forgotten that it's Oscar's birthday next week. I've invited a few friends to a surprise party for Oscar, but they (2) haven't answered. I know that Freddie has looked for a good present for Oscar but he (3) hasn't found anything. And Olivia (4) hasn't thought of anything. I've talked to Oscar's parents: They (5) haven't decided what party games we can play. And I know that Oscar's grandma has started knitting some socks but she (6) hasn't finished them. So I hope we'll all be ready on the day!

9 LANGUAGE Present perfect Ready for Oscar's birthday

▶ More help, p. 68 ▶ SB, p. 109

Write the verbs in the present perfect: *has* or *have* + past participle.
Note: The past participles all have regular forms.

1 Oscar's parents have prepared (prepare) a few games.

2 Oscar's grandma has knitted (knit) a pair of socks.

3 Freddie has remembered (remember) to buy a present.

4 Olivia has helped (help) to make a birthday cake.

5 Ling and her friends have planned (plan) a surprise party.

6 And they have invited (invite) a few of Oscar's best friends.

!

Be careful with one syllable[1] verbs that end with a consonant:

knit – I've knitted

plan – she has planned

[1] **syllable** *Silbe*

10 LANGUAGE Past participles

► SB, p. 110

Write the past participles of the verbs.

1 I have (do)
2 we have (get)
3 they have (come)
4 he has (forget)
5 we haven't (see)
6 she hasn't (sleep)
7 you have (make)
8 he has (think)
9 they have (have)
10 we haven't (send)
11 I've (hear)
12 she has (find)
13 they have (buy)
14 we have (knit)

11 LANGUAGE Present perfect Oscar's birthday

► More help, p. 68 ► SB, p. 110

Oscar is having a great birthday. What does he say? Write the verbs in the present perfect.
Note: The past participles all have irregular forms.

1 Look! Olivia *has made* (make) an amazing birthday cake.

2 And Freddie *has found* (find) a really funny costume.

3 Mum and Dad *have had* (have) some great ideas for party games.

4 And I*'ve got* (get) some nice winter socks from Grandma.

5 And Ling, you *have thought* (think) of so many things!

6 You *have* all *done* (do) so much for me.
Thank you for everything!

Erklär-film

12 LANGUAGE Present perfect: yes/no-questions

▶ More help, p. 69 ▶ SB, p. 111

Look at the list. Then complete the questions and answers. Question 6 is a trick question ☺ !

1 Has Meera decorated the cake yet?
– No, she hasn't.

2 Have Ben and Willow finished the wedding song?
– Yes, they have.

3 Has Meera bought enough drinks?
– Yes, she has.

4 Have Sunita and Nish tidied the living room?
– No, they haven't.

5 Has Ben found a tie for the wedding day? – Yes, he has.

6 And you, Willow. Have you forgotten to put out the rubbish?
– No, I haven't! I have done it!

1 Decorate the cake. ✗
2 Finish the wedding song. ✓
3 Buy enough drinks. ✓
4 Tidy the living room. ✗
5 Find a tie for the big day. ✓
6 Put out the rubbish. ✓

tidy → I've tidied

13 SPEAKING Game in class

▶ Digital help ▶ SB, p. 111

When the game starts, ask a student in class a question.
If he/she answers 'No, I haven't.', ask a different question.
If he/she answers 'Yes, I have.', write the student's name – and swap roles.
When both partners have finished, go to a different student and ask more questions.
You win if you are the first person with all 9 names or if you have the most names after 10 minutes.

1 Have you ever travelled to Italy? Yes? Name: ________	2 Have you ever made a funny costume? Yes? Name: ________	3 Have you ever eaten fish and chips? Yes? Name: ________
4 Have you ever seen a famous film or music star? Yes? Name: ________	5 Have you ever bought a cycling helmet? Yes? Name: ________	6 Have you ever lived in a country outside Germany? Yes? Name: ________
7 Have you ever slept till 12 o'clock? Yes? Name: ________	8 Have you ever played table tennis? Yes? Name: ________	9 Have you ever had a night in hospital? Yes? Name: ________

I can talk about preparations and experiences.

14 Oscar's train ticket

► SB, p. 113

a) **Complete the sentences. Use:** any- / every- / no- / some- + -where

b) **Complete the sentences. Use:** any- / every- / no- / some- + -one / -thing / -where

c) **Act out the scene in a group of three.**

15 LISTENING A dangerous Guy Fawkes party

▶ SB, p. 113

18

a) **Listen to Ling's story and answer the questions.**

1 Who had an accident: *Ling*

2 Where did it happen? *In the living room / in a neighbour's house*

18

b) **Now listen again and tick (✓) the correct answer A–D.**

1 Where did the party start?

- A inside ☐
- B outside ☑
- C inside and outside ☐
- D at Ling's school ☐

2 It was cold, so Ling

- A wore warm clothes. ☑
- B stayed inside. ☐
- C went home early. ☐
- D borrowed warm clothes. ☐

3 Danielle asked people to move back so that

- A everyone could see the fireworks. ☐
- B everyone could get sausages. ☐
- C everyone could help with the fireworks. ☐
- D everyone was safe. ☑

4 When everyone went inside,

- A there was a big meal. ☐
- B the house was hot and full. ☑
- C everyone was in one big room. ☐
- D everyone was really cold. ☐

5 How did Oscar stop the fire? He

- A hit Ling's dress. ☑
- B phoned for a fire engine. ☐
- C went to find water. ☐
- D knocked the candle off the table. ☐

6 At the end of the story, Oscar

- A gave Ling his jacket. ☐
- B was a bit scared. ☐
- C was angry with Danielle. ☑
- D joked about the fire. ☐

c) **What do YOU think?**

1 What do you think the strange smell was? *Ling's dress was on fire.*

2 What was dangerous in the house? *Candles with lots of people.*

3 Was Danielle careful? *Yes, she was careful outside, but not inside.*

▶ Challenge 1, p. 69

I can **talk about family celebrations.**

16 READING Tell the story

▶ SB, pp. 114–116

Put the sentences in the correct order. Write 2–10 in the boxes.

- [4] A Two men steal the bikes.
- [3] B Willow shows Ben the wedding bikes.
- [8] C Ben goes to his wedding in slippers.
- [1] D Ben gets up and puts on his slippers.
- [10] E Meera laughs when she hears what has happened.
- [9] I Ben is worried that Meera will be disappointed.
- [5] F Ben and Willow run downstairs and out into the street.
- [6] G The door of Ben and Willow's house suddenly closes.
- [2] J Ben asks Willow about a taxi.
- [7] H Ben can't get his phone or his money because they're in the flat.

17 MEDIATION Help a friend

▶ Digital help ▶ SB, pp. 114–116

After school a friend writes to you because he/she doesn't understand the story. He/She asks you to explain in German what happened in the story. Write no more than 10 sentences.

(In der Geschichte geht es um die Hochzeit von Ben und Meera. Am Anfang helfen Sunita, Nish und Willow ihren Eltern bei den Vorbereitungen. Sunita macht sich Sorgen, dass Ben zu spät zur Hochzeit kommt, aber Willow beruhigt sie. Willow überrascht ihren Vater mit dekorierten Fahrrädern, doch in dem Moment werden diese gestohlen. Ben und Willow rennen nach unten, doch die Fahrräder sind weg und sie haben sich ausgeschlossen. Ohne Handy und in Hausschuhen macht sich Ben gemeinsam mit Willow auf den Weg zur Hochzeit. Ben macht sich Sorgen, dass Meera enttäuscht von ihm ist. Aber am Ende macht es ihr nichts aus, dass er zu spät ist und Hausschuhe anhat, denn sie freut sich nur.)

▶ Challenge 2, p. 69

I can talk about different cultures in my life. ✓

18 Words in Unit 4

Match the words 1–6 with the meanings A–F.

1 awake D 2 both F 3 on time C

4 poor A 5 sick B 6 strange E

A with only a little money
B not healthy
C not late
D not asleep
E weird
F two of them

19 Food

▸ Digital help

a) Look at the pictures and write the words in the puzzle. 7 a + b = two words.

1 
apple ...

2 

3 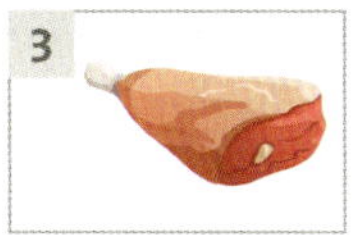
meat from a pig

4 

5 

6 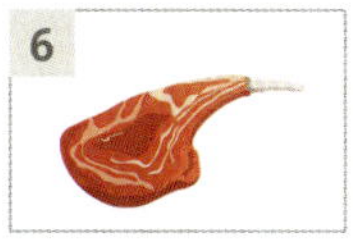
meat from a sheep

7 
a + b

8 

9 
meat from a cow

1	2	3	4	5	6	7a	8	9	7b
							B		
							I		
							S		B
J	Y		P				C		E
U	O		A				U	B	A
I	G	P	N	S		B	I	E	N
C	H	O	C	O	L	A	T	E	S
E	U	R	A	U	A	K		F	
	R	K	K	P	M	E			
	T		E		B	D			

b) Complete the phrases with the word in blue and other words from the puzzle.

1 a box of biscuits/chocolates
2 a pot of yoghurt
3 a carton of juice
4 A tin of baked beans
5 a few biscuits/pancakes
6 a little (beef/lamb/pork/soup/ ...)

20 SPEAKING Speak English well: When you're happy about something

19 **a) Oscar is having dinner at Ling's house. Listen to his sentences.**

Can you hear it? To sound polite and enthusiastic[1] the intonation goes **up** in the important words of the sentence.

1 I'm (↗ REALLY) (↗ HAPPY) to be here.
2 It's so (↗ KIND) of you!
3 The food is (↗ REALLY) nice. (↗ THANK) you.
4 This is an am-(↗ A)-zing dessert!
5 That was a fan-(↗ TAS)-tic meal. (↗ THANK) you.

20 **b) Listen and repeat the sentences in a). Be as polite and enthusiastic as you can!**

[1] **enthusiastic** *begeistert*

The big event in Unit 4 in my book: Meera and Ben's wedding

Things for a celebration:

good food, (candles)

(balloons)

(drinks)

What I know about Guy Fawkes night:

(bonfire, fireworks, ...)

What I know about Eid al-Fitr:

(break the fast, give money to charity, ...)

I remember:

words for food and drinks: (eggs, cream, beef, lamb, honey, apple juice, biscuits, ...)

how to say how much: a packet of, (a pot of, a bottle of, a tin of, a jar of, a carton of)

some irregular past participles: I've met, (seen, thought, sent, bought, found, ...)

3 words with *any/some/no*: (anywhere, someone, nothing, ...)

I can write full sentences with:

some and *any*: (I have some money. / Do you have any money? / I don't have any money. / ...)

a few and *a little*: (I have a few tomatoes. / I need a little bread. / ...)

the present perfect: (I've tidied my room. / ...)

questions and answers with *ever*: (Have you ever made a cake? – No, I haven't. / ...)

My progress[1] in English:

☐ very good ☐ quite good

☐ slower than I want!

Slow progress?
Practise a little every day!

[1] **progress** *Fortschritt*

Early finisher 1 Bank holidays in England

a) Use the internet and list the bank holidays in England.

New Year's Day, Good Friday, Easter Monday,

May Bank Holiday,

Spring Bank Holiday,

Summer Bank Holiday,

Christmas Day, Boxing Day

- In Britain the days when people get a holiday and don't go to work are called **bank holidays**.
- There are more bank holidays in Scotland and Northern Ireland than in England.
- If a bank holiday is on a Saturday or Sunday, then the next Monday becomes a bank holiday (so the bank holiday isn't 'lost').

b) Look at the box in a). What's the difference between bank holidays and holidays in Germany?

If a holiday is on a Saturday or Sunday, then the people in Germany lose that holiday.

▶ Check

Early finisher 2 Celebrations

a) Read the sentences about Ramadan in Zane's family. Then write the correct words in the sentences.

about | because | between | but | during | for | from | in | of | to

(1) During Ramadan Zane's dad doesn't eat (2) between sunrise and sunset. He works (3) in a cafe so of course it's hard (4) for him. (5) But he fasts (6) because it is important to him. The rest (7) of the family doesn't fast. Eid al-Fitr isn't just (8) about coming together and celebrating. Zane's parents give money (9) to charity and Zane often gets presents (10) from his grandparents.

▶ Check

b) Now think of your favourite meal. Write a shopping list for it.

▶ Digital help

My favourite meal is: ______________

____

Shopping list

____

____

____

____

____

____

____

2 More help One after the other

▶ WB, p. 56 ▶ SB, p. 103

Write the words in blue in the correct order.

1 twenty, *thirty, forty, fifty* (forty, thirty, fifty)

2 March, *April, May, June* (June, April, May)

3 spring, *summer, autumn, winter* (winter, autumn, summer)

4 six o'clock, *quarter past six, half past six, quarter to eight* (quarter to eight, half past six, quarter past six)

9 More help LANGUAGE Ready for Oscar's birthday

▶ WB, p. 59 ▶ SB, p. 109

Write the verbs in the present perfect: *has* or *have* + past participle.
Note: The past participles are all regular.

1 Oscar's parents *have prepared* (prepare) a few games.

2 Oscar's grandma *has knitted* (knit) a pair of socks.

3 Freddie *has remembered* (remember) to buy a present.

4 Olivia *has helped* (help) to make a birthday cake.

5 Ling and her friends *have planned* (plan) a surprise party.

6 And they *have invited* (invite) a few of Oscar's best friends.

!

Be careful with one syllable[1] verbs that end with one consonant:
knit – I've knitted
plan – she has planned

11 More help LANGUAGE Oscar's birthday

▶ WB, p. 60 ▶ SB, p. 110

Oscar is having a great birthday. What does he say? Write the verbs in the present perfect.
Note: The past participles all have irregular forms.

1 Look! Olivia *has m a d e* (make) an amazing birthday cake.

2 And Freddie *has f o u n d* (find) a really funny costume.

3 Mum and Dad *have h a d* (have) some great ideas for party games.

4 And I*'ve g o t* (get) some nice winter socks from Grandma.

5 And Ling, you *have t h o u g h t* (think) of so many things!

6 You *have* all *d o n e* (do) so much for me. Thank you for everything!

[1] **syllable** *Silbe*

12 More help LANGUAGE Preparing for the wedding

▶ WB, p. 61 ▶ SB, p. 111

Look at the list and answer the questions. Question 6 is a trick question ☺ !

1 Has Meera decorated the cake yet? – No, she hasn't.

2 Have Ben and Willow finished the wedding song?

– Yes, they have.

3 Has Meera bought enough drinks? – Yes, she has.

4 Have Sunita and Nish tidied the living room?

– No, they haven't.

5 Has Ben found a tie for the wedding day? – Yes, he has.

6 And you, Willow. Have you forgotten to put out the rubbish? – No, I haven't! I've done it!

1 Decorate the cake. ✗
2 Finish the wedding song. ✓
3 Buy enough drinks. ✓
4 Tidy the living room. ✗
5 Find a tie for the big day. ✓
6 Put out the rubbish. ✓

Challenge 1 A celebration in my family

▶ WB, p. 63

Write about a celebration in your family. Use some of the ideas below or your own ideas.

We all meet in/at ... We sing ... We eat... My dad / My mum prepares ... I feel ... because ...

Name of the celebration: ____________________ When is it? ____________________

____

____

____

____

Challenge 2 Ben on his wedding day

▶ WB, p. 64

Complete the sentences with the correct verbs from the box. Use the simple past.

be • feel • laugh • put • run • say • see • steal • ~~wear~~

Ben (1) wore a suit and (2) put on a tie. But two men (3) stole Ben and Willow's bikes. So Ben and Willow (4) ran into the street. But Ben's keys and phone (5) were still in the flat. 'I can't phone anyone,' (6) said Ben. That's why Ben (7) felt sad when he walked to his wedding. But Meera only (8) laughed when she (9) saw Ben's slippers. ▶ Check

1 Food words

a) Match the words from the first box with the food words from the second box. ▸ Digital help

~~bottle~~ • box • jar • packet • piece • pot • tin

baked beans • cheese • chocolates • honey • lemonade • strawberry yoghurt • tea

1 a bottle of lemonade

2 a box of chocolates

3 a jar of honey

4 a packet of tea

5 a piece of cheese

6 a pot of strawberry yoghurt

7 a tin of baked beans

b) Now write the different sorts of meat.

1  lamb

2  pork

3  beef

4  chicken

5  ham

6  sausage

2 How much?

Erklär-film

a) Mum is asking Callum to buy a few things in the shop. Complete the text with *some* or *any*.

Can you go to the shop for me, please, Callum? We need (1) some *bread and (2)* some *baked beans. And, wait a moment ... we don't need (3)* any *cheese but could you get me (4)* some *butter, please. And, why not, buy (5)* some *biscuits. But don't get (6)* any *cake – I'm going to make a cake tomorrow. Oh yes, get (7)* some *sugar for the cake. But we don't need (8)* any *flour.*

b) Look at what Callum's mum uses to make her cake. Write the words from the box with *a little* or *a few*.

~~butter~~ • eggs • flour • milk • pieces of chocolate • sugar

She needs a little butter, a few eggs, a little flour, a little milk, a few pieces of chocolate and a little sugar.

▸ Check

3 Irregular verbs in the present perfect

▶ Digital help

a) Look at the verbs in the box. Write the six past participles that end in -EN or -EEN.

be • blow • buy • come • eat • feed • find • forget • get • hear • lose • make • meet • put • ride • see • send • set • sing • steal • swim • think • wear

We have (1) been, I've (2) eaten,

I've (3) forgotten, she has (4) ridden,

they have (5) seen, he has (6) stolen.

If you need help, check on page 242 of your book.

b) Now write the past participles of the other verbs in the box that you write with:

1 O (not OU): it has blown, I've come, she has got, we have lost, they have worn

2 U: we have put, he has sung, they have swum

3 E (not EA): she has fed, we have met, he has sent, you have set

4 OUGHT: I've bought, she has thought

c) Write the three past participles which were not in a) or b).

I've found, we have heard, he has made

Erklär-film

4 Celebrations

▶ Digital help

a) Answer the questions.

1 Have you ever made a birthday cake?

Yes, I have. / No, I haven't.

2 Has your birthday ever been in a school holiday? Yes, it has. / No, it hasn't.

3 Have your friends ever given you a really bad present? Yes, they have. / No, they haven't.

!

question	short answer
Has he answered?	Yes, he has. / No, he hasn't.
Have you eaten?	Yes, I have. / No, I haven't.

b) Now complete Tia's text with the verbs in the present perfect.

My sister was born on Christmas Day so she (1) hasn't ever celebrated (not / ever / celebrate) her birthday on the right day. She (2) has always had (always / have) her birthday party in June. That's when my parents (3) have always bought (always / buy) or (4) made (make) her presents. (5) I've often had (often / have) my birthday party a few days after my real birthday. But I (6) haven't ever had (not / ever / have) a birthday six months late, like my sister. ▶ Check

Unit 5
Getting ready for the future

1 Looking at the pictures

► SB, p. 133

Look at the pictures on pages 132 and 133 in your book. Then write the correct letters below.

The person in the picture ...

1 isn't standing or sitting. C
2 is wearing a yellow helmet. E
3 is wearing red trousers. H
4 is working on a car. F
5 is working with food. G
6 is wearing a face mask. D
7 is cutting hair. B
8 is using water. C
9 is working in front of a mirror. B

2 Lots of different jobs

► SB, p. 133

a) **Complete the sentences with words from the box. Remember:** *I'm + a / an + job.*

artist • builder • cook • firefighter • hairdresser • mechanic • nurse • programmer

1 *I paint, draw or make other forms of art.* I'm an artist.

2 *I work in a team – we make new buildings.* I'm a builder.

3 *I work on cars when they don't work.* I'm a mechanic.

4 *I make new computer programs.* I'm a programmer.

5 *I look after people.* I'm a nurse.

6 *I cut people's hair.* I'm a hairdresser.

7 *I prepare meals.* I'm a cook.

8 *I fight fires.* I'm a firefighter.

b) **Many jobs end in *-er*. Write the jobs.**

1 I swim – I'm a swimmer.
2 I drive ambulances – I'm an ambulance driver.
3 I teach – I'm a teacher.
4 I read the news on TV – I'm a news reader.
5 I clean rooms – I'm a cleaner.
6 I play basketball – I'm a basketball player.

I can talk about jobs.

3 Language Word order Future jobs

▸ More help, p. 84 ▸ SB, p. 134

a) Read the tip about the word order in English.

	subject	verb	object
Word order in English is	I	want to be	a programmer.

b) Now read the German sentences and complete the English translations.

1 Ich will Zugfahrer werden, weil ich Züge mag.

I	*want to be*	*a train driver,*	because	*I*	*like*	*trains.*

2 Später will ich Menschen helfen. Vielleicht kann ich Krankenpfleger werden.

Later	*I*	*want to help*	*people.*	Maybe	*I*	*can be*	*a nurse.*

3 Als ich klein war, wollte ich Mechanikerin werden. Jetzt will ich Architektin werden.

When	*I*	*was*	*little,*	*I*	*wanted to be*	*a mechanic.*
Now	*I*	*want to be*	*an architect.*			

4 Listening Different dreams

21

▸ SB, p. 135

a) Look at the jobs A–G. Then listen to five teenagers and match them with a job. Write the correct letter A–G next to the name. You don't need all the jobs.

b) Listen again, and write why they chose this job.

	Name	Job	Why?
1	Muhammad	*D*	loves *drawing houses*
2	Isla	*G*	good with *animals*
3	Leo	*F*	interested in[1] *bikes and cars*
4	Freya	*B*	wants to really *understand* computers
5	Archie	*E*	wants to work *in a hospital, in a team*

A police officer
B programmer
C builder
D architect
E nurse
F mechanic
G vet

c) Now check your answers with a partner.

Muhammad wants to be ... because, ... | *Yes, that's right.* | *No, that's wrong. He wants to be ...*

[1] **be interested in** *sich für etwas interessieren*

5 LANGUAGE Will-future The weather tomorrow

► SB, p. 136

Erklärfilm

Look at the online weather forecast[1] for York tomorrow. Then (circle) *will* or *won't* in the sentences.

1 It says it **will / won't** be sunny tomorrow.
2 It says it **will / won't** rain tomorrow.
3 But it **will / won't** be windy.
4 It says it **will / won't** snow tomorrow.
5 It **will / won't** be warm tomorrow.
6 It **will / won't** be cold tomorrow.

6 LANGUAGE Will-future Oscar and Ling

► Digital help ► SB, p. 136

What will Oscar and Ling do on Saturday? Write sentences with *will* or *won't*.

1 Oscar / tidy / his room
2 He / go / shopping
3 He / meet / some friends / in town
4 He / have dinner / in town
5 Ling / go / swimming
6 She / buy / any new trousers
7 She / meet / Oscar
8 She / get / a book / from the library

yes, yes, no, no, yes, yes, no, no

1 Oscar will tidy his room.
2 He won't go shopping.
3 He will meet some friends in town.
4 He won't have dinner in town.
5 Ling will go swimming.
6 She won't buy any new trousers.
7 She won't meet Oscar.
8 She will get a book from the library.

[1] **forecast** *Vorhersage*

7 LANGUAGE Will-future Getting ready for a hike

▶ SB, p. 137

Oscar is getting ready for a hike. Write *'ll* or *won't*.

I'm going to go hiking in the hills today. It's hot today, so I'll (1) need something to drink but I won't (2) need warm clothes. My friends Andy and Valeria are going to come with me, so I won't (3) be alone. I'll (4) need some money for the bus ticket home, of course. But I won't (5) need a map because Valeria has a map app. There's a nice river on our way so I'll (6) take my swimming things. And I'm always hungry when I go hiking so I'll (7) take some sandwiches, some fruit and some chocolate. I want to be sure that I won't (8) be hungry this time!

8 LANGUAGE Will-future A weekend in London

▶ SB, p. 137

Ling is talking to her cousin Flora. Write *will*, *'ll* or *won't* + the correct verb.

be • buy • do • eat • go • have • see • spend • take • ~~travel~~ • visit

Ling You're all going to London this weekend, aren't you?

Flora Yes, we'll travel (1) to London by train on Saturday morning.

Ling Do you know what you'll do (2) in London?

Flora Well, we won't see (3) all the sights, because we won't have (4) that much time. But we'll go (5) to Buckingham Palace and we'll take (6) a walk in Hyde Park. We'll eat (7) something delicious at Camden Market, and perhaps I 'll buy (8) a cool T-shirt there.

Ling Anything else? Perhaps Madame Tussauds?

Flora No, we won't visit (9) Madame Tussauds. It's just too expensive. We 'll spend (10) our money on a show in the evening.

Ling And what about Sunday?

Flora My mum wants to go to the National History Museum. I hope it won't be (11) too boring.

▶ Early finisher 1, p. 83 ▶ Challenge 1, p. 84

I can make predictions about my future.

9 The chores in Oscar's family

► SB, p. 138

Write the verbs in the simple present.

babysit • clean • cook • do • empty • fold • look • make • set • take • ~~tidy~~ • vacuum

Remember in the simple present:
He/she + verb + s
We see. → He sees.
They fry. → She fries. (consonant + y → -ies)

1 Oscar *tidies* his room when it's messy and he sometimes *cooks* the dinner.

2 Oscar's mum and dad *take* out the rubbish.

3 Oscar's dad *does* the washing and his mum or dad *cleans* the bathroom.

4 Freddie *empties* the dishwasher.

5 Olivia *sets* the table and Oscar's mum *vacuums* the floors.

6 Oscar's dad *folds* the clean clothes and they all *make* their own beds.

7 Oscar often *babysits* at his neighbour's house and they all *look* after the family cat.

10 When are you free?

► SB, p. 139

Partner B: look at page 87.

a) **Partner A: You want to meet Partner B after school. Ask if he/she is free after school. If yes, write 'free'. If no, write why.**

Are you free after school on Monday/Tuesday/...?

Monday	Tuesday	Wednesday	Thursday	Friday
free	*walk the dog*	*football club*	*clean bathroom*	*free*

b) **Now look at your plans for the week. Then listen to your partner and answer him/her.**

Yes, I'm free.

No, sorry, I always ... on Monday/Tuesday/ ...

Monday	Tuesday	Wednesday	Thursday	Friday
 dinner	*free*	 lesson	 floors	*free*

c) **Now compare your information. On which day can you meet after school?** *Friday*

11 The morning routine

▸ More help, p. 85 ▸ SB, p. 139

Complete the text with the correct verb: *has to / have to / doesn't have to / don't have to*

On school days I (1) don't have to get up till quarter past seven. Mum and Dad (2) have to get up earlier because they need more time in the bathroom. We have a quick breakfast, because Mum (3) has to leave the house at quarter to eight. Dad (4) has to be at work at half past eight, so he (5) doesn't have to leave till eight o'clock. And my sister and I have more time too. We (6) don't have to leave the house till quarter past eight. School starts at ten to nine, but we only (7) have to be there at 8.40.

12 A takeaway dinner

▸ Digital help ▸ SB, p. 140

Oscar's family is going to get a takeaway Indian meal this evening. Read the dialogue and circle the correct option.

A takeaway meal is when a restaurant brings a meal to your house or you pick it up at the restaurant.

Mum Hooray! We (1) **don't have to / mustn't** make dinner this evening because we're going to have a takeaway meal. Here's the menu ... now, what do we want to get?

Oscar Remember, Olivia is vegetarian so we (2) **don't have to / mustn't** get a meat dish for her. And we (3) **don't have to / mustn't** forget to get mattar paneer for Dad – it's his favourite dish!

Mum I think we have enough rice from last night, so we (4) **don't have to / mustn't** get any more. OK, I'll message the restaurant.

Oscar There's no school tomorrow, so I (5) **don't have to / mustn't** do any homework before the meal!

Mum OK, but Oscar, we want to hear the people when they bring the food, so you (6) **don't have to / mustn't** make too much noise!

13 LISTENING A house in Wales

22

▸ SB, p. 140

Oscar is going to stay with his family in Aunt Jane's house in Wales. Listen to Aunt Jane. What can / can't they do in the house? Write ✓ or ✗.

Use the hot water	✓
Open the bathroom window	✗
Use the dishwasher	✗
Leave food in the kitchen	✓
Bring a dog	✗
Make lots of noise	✓

I can talk about chores.

14 Money

▶ SB, p. 140

Complete the sentences with words from the box.

coins • earn • machine • money • need • pocket • presents • put • save • spend

How money comes in:

– You get (1) pocket money from your parents in cash.

– Your parents use a pocket money app and (2) put money on a card every month.

– You (3) earn money when you do chores for people.

– You get (4) money on special days, like holidays or your birthday.

– You have a card and get money from a cash (5) machine.

How money goes out:

– You buy things you (6) need (like clothes) and things you like (like chocolate and games).

– You (7) spend money on treats like going to a movie or going bowling.

– You buy (8) presents for your friends and family.

– You (9) save your money for later in a savings account.

– If you don't need them now, you put (10) coins in a piggy bank at home.

15 LANGUAGE Adverbs of manner

▶ Digital help ▶ SB, p. 141

a) **Write the adjectives or adverbs.**

Adjective	Adverb
Lara is confident.	She talks confidently.
Karim is quiet.	He talks quietly.
Jan is angry.	He talks angrily.
Ayami is loud.	She talks loudly.
Emily is kind.	She talks kindly.
Elena is happy.	She talks happily.
Josh is careful.	He talks carefully.

Remember: Adverbs of manner describe how you do something:
I dress comfortab**ly**.
We always listen careful**ly**.

!
Note these special forms:
angry → angr**ily**
careful → careful**ly**

b) **Karim has a new job. Write the adjectives or adverbs.**

My new job started (1) badly (bad). The work wasn't (2) easy (easy) and I didn't speak (3) politely (polite) to the customers. But now I'm (4) happy (happy) here, and I'm working (5) happily (happy) and (6) successfully (successful).

▶ Challenge 2, p. 85

16 Mediation Saturdays

▶ SB, p. 141

Mediate for Vera, a German friend who wants to meet an English friend, Olivia. Write your sentences below.

Remember: In English you say the place before the time. P comes before T in the alphabet.

Vera Können wir uns am Samstag im Park treffen?

You Can we meet *in the park on Saturday?*

Olivia OK. Where in the park? And at what time?

You OK. *Wo im Park?* Und *um wieviel Uhr?*

Vera Sagen wir um halb drei im Café?

You Let's say *in the cafe at half past two?*

Olivia Yes, that's fine. But I'll have to be home two hours later.

You Prima. Aber sie *muss zwei Stunden später zu Hause sein.*

17 Shopping for clothes

▶ More help, p. 85 ▶ SB p. 143

a) **Jo is talking to a shop assistant (SA). Read dialogue 1 with a partner.**

b) **Complete dialogue 2. Use the plural forms for the words in yellow.**

c) **Listen and check.** 23

d) **Then read dialogue 2 with a partner.**

1 Buying a T-shirt	2 Buying trousers
Jo What size is this T-shirt?	**Jo** What size *are* *these* trousers?
SA It's size M.	**SA** *They're* size M.
Jo Do you have it in blue?	**Jo** Do you have *them* in blue?
SA No, we don't. But that T-shirt is blue. Is it OK?	**SA** No, we don't. But *those* trousers are blue. *Are* *they* OK?
Jo Great. Can I try it on?	**Jo** Great. Can I try *them* on?
SA Yes, of course.	**SA** Yes, of course.
Jo How much does it cost?	**Jo** How much *do* *they* cost?
SA £12.99.	**SA** £38.99.
Jo It's perfect. I'll take it.	**Jo** *They're* perfect. I'll take *them*.

I can talk about money and shopping.

18 Tell the story of the video

► SB, p. 147

a) **Match the people and the actions A–F. A person can have one or more actions.**

A nearly breaks something | B washed the clothes | C is at home | D keeps the time | E folds the clothes best | F talks like an announcer[1]

Emir C, F Daisy A Gloria D Joe E Emir's dad B

b) **Now check your answers with a partner.**

I think Emir ... *Yes, I agree.* *Really? I don't think so. I think Emir ...*

c) VIEWING **Now watch the video, and check your answers.**

19 VIEWING What's the missing word?

► SB, p. 147

Watch the video and write the missing words.

Part 1 (00:31 to 01:02)

1 Emir: 'Dad says I can't go out until I finish doing my chores.'

Part 2 (01:03 to 01:47)

2 Emir: 'I need to fold them before I can go out.'

3 Joe: 'Who wants to try?'

Part 3 (01:48 to 03:30)

4 Emir: 'He's fast. But can he be tidy?'

Part 4 (03:31 to 03:54)

5 Gloria: 'Oops! Don't break anything!'

6 Emir: 'Do you think they will also do my homework?'

20 Opinions

► SB, p. 147

Complete sentences 1 and 2. Then write your own opinion in sentence 3.

1 Joe and Daisy are really kind because they help Emir with his chores.

2 Joe and Daisy are a bit stupid because they do Emir's work and Emir does nothing.

3 What do you think? ______

[1] **announcer** *Ansager/in*

21 Wrong word!

Which word is wrong? Why?
Use words from the box to say why.

chore • clothes • feeling • job • money • money verb • ~~shop~~ • treat

1 bakery office charity shop newsagent — *office* is wrong, because it isn't a *shop*.

2 builder nurse customer hairdresser — *customer* because it isn't a *job*.

3 clean tidy vacuum enjoy — *enjoy* because it isn't a *chore*.

4 size change cash coin — *size* because it isn't *money*.

5 embarrassed famous angry surprised — *famous* because it isn't a *feeling*.

6 bowls shorts trousers suits — *bowls* because they aren't *clothes*.

7 gift chore screen time movie — *chore* because it isn't a *treat*.

8 save mind spend buy — *mind* because it isn't a *money verb*.

22 Silent letters

a) **In the words below, highlight the letters that you don't say.**

business	builder	comfortable	mechanic	receipt	spotlight

24 b) **Listen and check your answers.**

c) **Now say the words to your partner. Then swap roles.**

23 Speak English well: TH

25 a) **Voiced TH**

Listen and repeat the words.
Tip: You can't whisper a voiced TH!

they, there, these, mother, another

I clean the windows and vacuum the floor.

26 b) **Unvoiced TH**

Listen and repeat the words.

teeth, thirty, thing, birthday

Think of your health!

27 c) **Listen and repeat: voiced and unvoiced**

1 Don't think too long about these things!

2 Both my brothers like buying clothes.

Voiced TH [ð] usually:
Start of function words: this, the, those, then
Middle of words: father, other
A difficult one: clothes

Unvoiced TH [θ] usually:
End of words: strength, north, month, health
Start of non-function words: think, theatre, three

Shhh! I'll tell you a secret: not everyone in Britain can say a TH! Some say 'vis', not 'this', or 'maffs' not 'maths'. So try to say TH – but it isn't tragic if you can't ☺.

The story in Unit 5:

My favourite character(s) in the story:

__________ because __________

I liked / didn't like the story in Unit 5 because __________

Some long words in Unit 5:

dishwasher

(firefighter)

(successful)

(comfortable)

Jobs:

(builder, architect, police officer, manager, nurse, firefighter, programmer, hairdresser, mechanic, ...)

I remember different chores: I *(set the table, empty the dishwasher, take out the rubbish, clean the bathroom, wash/fold the clothes, babysit, ...)*

I can write a sentence with

- *will*: *(It will rain tomorrow.)*
- *won't*: *(I won't be famous.)*
- *mustn't*: *(I mustn't be rude.)*
- *don't have to*: *(You don't have to give me a present.)*
- *this/that*: *(I like this tie, I don't like that tie.)*
- *these/those*: *(I like these trousers, not those trousers.)*
- an adverb with -LY: *(I run slowly, I read carefully.)*
- time and place in the correct order: *(I go there every day.)*

What I can do better in English next year:

☐ reading ☐ writing ☐ listening ☐ speaking

Early finisher 1 The big predictions quiz

a) Tick (✓) one or more predictions about your future.

1 My predictions for when I'm older:

A I'll stay in my town. ☐
B I'll stay in Germany. ☐
C I'll live in a different country. ☐
D I'll live in many different countries. ☐

2 When I'm older:

A People won't use coins any more. ☐
B People won't use cars any more. ☐
C People will live more comfortably. ☐
D Robots will vacuum our houses. ☐

3 When I'm older:

A I'll have at least three children. ☐
B I won't get married. ☐
C I'll get married and have children. ☐
D I won't have any children. ☐

4 When I'm older:

A I'll earn a lot of money. ☐
B I'll save and buy my own house. ☐
C I'll travel around the world. ☐
D Money won't be too important for me. ☐

5 When I'm older:

A I'll be a hairdresser. ☐
B I'll be an artist. ☐
C I'll be a footballer. ☐
D I'll be famous. ☐
E Not A, B, C or D ☐

6 When I'm older:

A I want to have my own business. ☐
B I'll be a computer programmer. ☐
C I'll work in the movie industry. ☐
D I want a job where I can be creative. ☐
E Not A, B, C or D ☐

b) Now write one more prediction of your own:

When I'm older ____________________

c) Now compare with other students in class. Who has the most predictions the same as you?

____

☒ **3** More help LANGUAGE **Word order Future jobs** ► WB, p. 73 ► SB, p. 134

a) **Read the tip about word order in English.**

Word order in English is	subject	verb	object
	I	want to be	a programmer.

b) **Now read the German sentences and complete the English translations.**

1 Ich will Zugfahrer werden, weil ich Züge mag.

want to be / I / a train driver / trains / like / I

I	want to be	a train driver,	because	I	like	trains.

2 Später will ich Menschen helfen. Vielleicht kann ich Krankenpfleger werden.

want / I / people / to help / can / I / a nurse / be

Later	I	want to help	people.	Maybe	I	can be	a nurse.

3 Als ich klein war, wollte ich Mechanikerin werden. Jetzt will ich Architektin werden.

I / little / was / wanted / I / a mechanic / to be / want / I / an architect / to be

When	I	was	little,	I	wanted to be	a mechanic.
Now	I	want to be	an architect.			

Challenge 1 **What I'll do if ...** ► Digital help ► WB, p. 75

Write the *if*-sentences with the correct forms of the verbs.

1 weather / be / nice / we / have / a barbecue

If the weather is nice, we'll have a barbecue.

2 be / rainy / we / stay / at home

If it 's rainy, we'll stay at home.

3 If / mum / go / to town / I / go / with her

If mum goes to town, I'll go with her.

4 If / I / be / tired / I / go / to bed / early

If I'm tired, I'll go to bed early.

► Check

11 More help The morning routine

▸WB, p. 77 ▸SB, p. 139

Circle the correct form of *have to.*

On school days I (1) **don't have to** / **doesn't have to** get up at quarter past seven. Mum and Dad (2) **have to** / **has to** get up earlier because they need more time in the bathroom. We have a quick breakfast, because Mum (3) **have to** / **has to** leave the house at quarter to eight.

Dad (4) **have to** / **has to** be at work at half past eight, so he (5) **have to** / **doesn't have to** leave till eight o'clock. And my sister and I have more time too. We (6) **don't have to** / **doesn't have to** leave the house till quarter past eight. School starts at ten to nine, but we only (7) **have to** / **has to** be there at 8.40.

Challenge 2 WRITING How do you work at school?

▸Digital help ▸WB, p. 78

Write as many sentences as you can. Use words from the box, but turn the adjectives into adverbs.

always • never • often • sometimes • usually • confident • happy • quiet • slow • successful

I usually work confidently. I (usually work happily. / I never work slowly. / I sometimes work quietly. / ...)

17 More help Shopping for clothes

▸WB, p. 79 ▸SB, p. 143

a) **Read dialogue 1 with a partner.**

b) **Complete dialogue 2. Use the plural forms in the box for the words in yellow.**

23 c) **Listen and check.**

d) **Then read dialogue 2 with a partner.**

1 Buying a T-shirt	2 Buying trousers
(SA = shop assistant)	are (x2) • do • them (x3) • these • those • they (x2) • they're (x2)
Jo What size is this T-shirt?	**Jo** What size *are* *these* trousers?
SA It's size M.	**SA** *They're* size M.
Jo Do you have it in blue?	**Jo** Do you have *them* in blue?
SA No, we don't. But that T-shirt is blue. Is it OK?	**SA** No, we don't. But *those* trousers are blue. *Are* *they* OK?
Jo Great. Can I try it on?	**Jo** Great. Can I try *them* on?
SA Yes, of course.	**SA** Yes, of course.
Jo How much does it cost?	**Jo** How much *do* *they* cost?
SA £12.99.	**SA** £38.99.
Jo It's perfect. I'll take it.	**Jo** *They're* perfect. I'll take *them*.

Unit 1 Topic 2 | Exercise 9

▶ WB, p. 12 ▶ SB, p. 19

a) **Partner B: Look at the information and read the train station announcements[1].**

The next train to Brighton is at 14.13 at platform 2. Platform 2 for the 14.13 train to Brighton.

The next train to … is at … at platform … Platform … for the … train to …

The next train …

Brighton 14.13	Platform 2
Hastings 14.21	Platform 5
Eastbourne 14.03	Platform 5
Portsmouth 14.09	Platform 4

b) **The train to Brighton is late. Look at the information and answer your partner's question.**

I'm sorry, the 14.13 train to Brighton is late. The new arrival time is … And it doesn't arrive at platform …, but at platform …

Brighton 14.13	Platform 2
New arrival time:	14.45
Platform change:	Platform 1

c) **Now listen to your partner. Write the times of the trains.**

Train to Woking: 19.05

Train to Gatwick Airport: 18.48

Train to Epsom: 18.59

Train to Dorking: 19.12

d) **Now ask your partner about the train to Dorking. Write the answer.**

Excuse me, please. Do I need to change trains for Dorking?

Answer: Yes, I need to change in Redhill.

e) **Now check your answers with your partner.**

[1] **announcement** *Ansage*

Unit 4 Topic 1 | Exercise 4

▸ WB, p. 57 ▸ SB, p. 106

a) Partner B: Look at what you have for your picnic. Then listen to your partner and answer.

Yes, I do. *No, sorry, I don't.*

 ✓
 ✗
 ✓
 ✓
 ✗
 ✓

b) Now ask your partner if he/she has these things for a picnic.
If yes, put a tick (✓). If no, put an ✗.

Do you have any ...?

carrots?	✓	apples?	✓
ham?	✗	cheese?	✗
orange juice?	✓	cake?	✓

c) Now write what you and your partner still need.

We still need some ham, some cheese, some yoghurt and some lemonade.

Unit 5 Topic 2 | Exercise 10

▸ WB. p. 76 ▸ SB, p. 139

a) Partner B: Partner A wants to meet you after school. Look at your plans for the week.
Listen to your partner and answer him/her.

Yes, I'm free. *No, sorry, I always ... on Monday/Tuesday/ ...*

Monday	Tuesday	Wednesday	Thursday	Friday
free		 club		free

b) Now ask your partner if he/she is free after school. If yes, write 'free'. If no, write why.

Are you free after school on Monday/Tuesday/...?

Monday	Tuesday	Wednesday	Thursday	Friday
cook dinner	free	guitar lesson	vacuum floors	free

c) Now compare your information. On which day can you meet after school? Friday

Typical tasks	Häufige Arbeitsanweisungen
Act out the conversation / part.	Führt das Gespräch / die Szene vor.
Answer the questions / partner B's questions.	Beantworte die Fragen / Partner/in Bs Fragen.
Ask questions.	Stelle Fragen.
Check with your partner.	Überprüfe mit deiner Partnerin / deinem Partner.
Choose the correct verbs / a person / ...	Wähle die richtigen Verben / eine Person / ...
Circle the right word / correct verb / ...	Kreise das richtige Wort / das richtige Verb / ... ein.
Compare the pictures / your answers / ... with a partner.	Vergleiche die Bilder / deine Antworten / ... mit einem/r Partner/in.
Complete the questions / message / ...	Vervollständige die Fragen / die Nachricht / ...
Correct the false / wrong sentences / answers.	Berichtige die falschen Sätze / Antworten.
Cross out the numbers / wrong things / ...	Streiche die Nummern / die falschen Dinge / ... durch.

Draw pictures / lines / ...	Zeichne / Male Bilder / Linien / ...
Fill the gaps with the right words.	Vervollständige die Lücken mit den richtigen Wörtern.
Find the answers / right picture / ...	Finde die Antworten / das richtige Bild / ...
Highlight the letters / words / ...	Markiere die Buchstaben / Wörter / ...
Listen again.	Höre nochmal zu.

Listen and check / read / write / ...	Höre zu und überprüfe / lies / schreibe / ...
Listen to the words / sentences / people / ...	Höre dir die Wörter / Sätze / Leute / ... an.
Look at the picture / answers / ...	Schau dir das Bild / die Antwort / ... an.
Match the pictures / ... with the sentences / ...	Ordne die Bilder / ... den Sätzen / ... zu.
Practise with a partner.	Übe mit einem/r Partner/in.
Put a cross in the box for the wrong sentences.	Setze ein Kreuzchen ins Kästchen für die falschen Sätze.
Put a tick in the box for the correct sentences / in the right boxes.	Setze ein Häkchen ins Kästchen für die richtigen Sätze / in die richtigen Kästchen.
Put the words in the right order.	Setze die Wörter in die richtige Reihenfolge.
Read about ...	Lies über ...
Read the messages / sentences / text / ...	Lies die Nachrichten / Sätze / den Text / ...
Right (✓) or wrong (✗)? / True (T) or false (F)?	Richtig oder falsch?
Swap roles.	Wechselt die Rollen.

Talk to a partner.	Sprich mit einem/r Partner/in.
Tick the correct definition / the hobbies / ...	Hake alle richtigen Definitionen / Hobbys / ... ab.
Underline ...	Unterstreiche ...
Use the answers / letters / ... from the box.	Benutze die Antworten / Buchstaben / ... aus dem Kasten.
Use words from the box.	Benutze die Wörter aus dem Kasten.
Watch part 1/2/... (again).	Sieh dir Teil 1/2/... (nochmal) an.
Write about six sports / your grandma / ...	Schreibe über sechs Sportarten / deine Oma / ...
Write the correct definitions / answers / sentences / ...	Schreibe die richtigen Definitionen / Antworten / Sätze / ...